# At the Spy's Pleasure

### an In the Crown's Secret Service novel

# At the Spy's Pleasure

*an In the Crown's Secret Service novel*

## TINA GABRIELLE

Entangled Publishing, LLC
2614 South Timberline Road
Suite 109
Fort Collins, CO 80525
Visit our website at www.entangledpublishing.com.

Scandalous is an imprint of Entangled Publishing, LLC.

Edited by Alycia Tornetta
Cover Design by Libby Murphy
Cover Art by Jenn LeBlanc / Illustrated Romance

ISBN 978-1-943336-31-9

Manufactured in the United States of America

First Edition May 2015

Scandalous
an Entangled imprint

*For John, with love.*

# Chapter One

JUNE 10, 1821
LONDON

*Tonight I will find a lover.*

Jane's pulse skittered with excitement as she stepped into the glittering ballroom. Tonight, for the first time, the widowed countess of Stanwell would abandon her mourning and find a man who could satisfy her needs, her secret desires, *her* pleasure.

Dozens of chandeliers holding hundreds of candles illuminated the ballroom. The elite of London society was present to celebrate the betrothal of the earl of Newbury's daughter to the Duke of Westmont. Jane knew the guests well. They were the same people she'd mingled with ever since her own debut ten years prior—aristocrats, powerful members of parliament, society hostesses, as well as the newest crop of debutantes and their marriage-minded mamas.

The same people who now smiled politely to her face and gossiped maliciously behind her back.

Jane wove through the crowd and halted by the refreshment table.

"Thank goodness you've finally discarded that horrid black."

The words came at her shoulder. Jane turned to find Lady Olivia, her close friend and the bride-to-be, smiling at her.

"I wouldn't call my mourning gowns horrid," Jane protested. Her current gown was deep purple, and she'd chosen it because the dressmaker insisted the rich shade accentuated her blond hair and fair complexion. Looking around the room, Jane realized her dress was still far from the vibrant colors of some of the other women's gowns.

"Well, I'm glad to see you're not in widow's weeds. It's been well over two years since Lord Stanwell's death. Tonight is my engagement ball, and I hope that your dance card will soon be filled," Olivia said.

Jane rolled her eyes. "Few gentlemen will approach to dance no matter how I'm garbed."

"You must give them a chance."

"I've tried. Society is not ready to forget." At Olivia's silence, Jane shrugged. "It makes no difference anymore. I've decided to take matters into my own hands."

Olivia's blue eyes widened. "What on earth does that mean?"

"Charles is gone. It's time I moved on."

Olivia smiled in approval. "I wholeheartedly agree. As your best friend, I've been praying for this day. Many eligible gentlemen are in attendance tonight. It's no secret Lord Bromley dislikes the notion of a fresh-faced debutante just out of the schoolroom."

Jane wrinkled her nose. "Not Bromley. He wants a wife."

"You don't want to remarry?"

*Never again.*

Jane leaned close and whispered. "I want a lover, not a suitor. And most definitely *not* a husband."

Olivia's mouth opened and closed, then she pulled Jane behind a potted palm. Glancing both ways to make certain they were not overheard, she spoke urgently, "A *lover*? You've been mostly secluded in your town home, suffering from melancholy, only wearing mourning gowns since… since…"

Olivia couldn't seem to say the words, so Jane took pity on her friend and said them for her. "Since Charles's suicide?"

Olivia swallowed. "Well, yes. And now you seek a lover?"

"Not just any lover. A skilled, experienced lover who has no interest in finding a wife."

Before Olivia could respond, Lady Newbury walked past their hidden spot calling for her eldest daughter. She was accompanied by the Dowager Duchess of Westmont, a tall woman with a long, bony face and sour expression.

"Your mother is searching for you," Jane said.

"Mother has been relentless tonight and insists on currying favor with the Dowager Duchess."

"The dowager seems taut as a bow."

"She's miserable and quite opinionated. She believes that at five and twenty, I'm too old to be marrying her grandson. She's demanded an heir and spare to the dukedom straightway, and measured my hips to see if they're sufficient to the task of child bearing."

Jane burst out laughing. "You're jesting!"

"I wish I were," Olivia said dryly.

"You don't have to marry the duke if—"

"No. It's not like that," Olivia said. "I adore Edward."

"And the dowager?" Jane asked.

"Will live in the dower house away from the main estate. But I've told Edward it doesn't matter where we live. I'd be happy in a country cottage as long as we are together. Despite what everyone thinks, I'm not marrying him to become a duchess."

Jane hugged Olivia. "Edward is the fortunate one."

Lady Newbury and the dowager strolled past once again. An anxious expression crossed Olivia's mother's face as she looked about the room for her wayward daughter.

"I must speak with them," Olivia said, with a meaningful look at Jane. "But I shall return quickly. We must talk about your shocking plan."

Olivia hurried off, and Jane remained behind the cover of the ornamental greenery. Scanning the ballroom, she spotted a group of relatively young gentlemen conversing. The men were bachelors and widowers, and any one of them would be eligible candidates as lovers, as she was seven and twenty.

Simon Marbury was particularly handsome, with a full head of fair hair and deep blue eyes. She wondered if he would be discreet enough to handle an illicit affair. He was known to care more about the folds in his cravat and the cut of his coat than intellectual pursuits, so she needn't worry about him delving into her soul. She had no intention of ever losing her heart or head to a man again.

The result had been disastrous.

A burst of laugher followed by hushed whispers from the nearby refreshment table drew her attention away from the men. Jane pushed aside a large palm frond to glimpse a group of ladies assembled by the punch bowl.

"Can you believe it? Lady Stanwell is present tonight and she's not wearing her customary black," a feminine voice said.

A giggle followed. "Perhaps she's husband hunting," a second lady said.

"What man would have her? After all, her husband shot himself in the head," a third woman added.

"And over a horse," said the first woman.

Jane froze as fingers of ice seeped into her every pore.

Oblivious to her presence, the women ruthlessly continued.

"She was first to find his body."

"Rumor has it she drove him to do the deed."

"She's cursed. No man will risk being with her."

Jane longed to spring from her hiding place to confront the malicious women face-to-face. She opened her mouth in dismay, but instead a suffocating sensation tightened her throat.

Her chest rose and fell with her labored breathing. The walls of the ballroom were closing in on her. Her bodice was too tight, her corset preventing any air from reaching her lungs. She felt light headed and ill.

This couldn't be happening. Not here, not tonight.

Not again.

She looked around frantically and her gaze homed in on the open French doors leading onto the terrace.

If she could make it so far…

Stepping from behind the palm, she rushed past the refreshment table and headed for the cool outdoors. Two, three, four… Eight more steps and she would make it.

She sucked the fresh night air into her lungs. The soft soles of her ballroom slippers were silent on the stone terrace. Hurrying to the ornate balustrade, her fingers wrapped around the iron.

After the brightly lit ballroom, the terrace was dim save for the garden torches below and the sliver of a half moon. She breathed deeply, her eyes adjusting to the dark, her heart rate slowing. The fragrant scent of rose bushes wafted to her. The barbs from the cruel and hurtful insults ebbed, but the ache in her chest did not completely ease.

She doubted the pain would ever entirely go away.

"Are you going to let them win so easily?"

Jane whirled at the masculine voice. She had thought the terrace was empty, but to her surprise she saw a man leaning against the doorway, legs crossed, arms folded... watching her. Candlelight from the ballroom behind him cast his features in shadow.

"Pardon?" she asked.

"Don't tell me you're going to let those magpies distress you?"

A sliver of alarm raced down her spine. "Who are you, sir?"

He stepped into the light from the torches. Jane sucked in a breath as recognition swept over her.

It couldn't be.

It was.

Gareth Ramsey.

Sweet Lord, up close he was a sight to behold. Just as she remembered. He was a barrister, the estranged son of Baron Suffolk. She had met him over a year ago when her cousin Sophia had married an earl, Lord Kirkland, who happened to be Gareth Ramsey's friend.

Amidst the refined gentlemen at the ball, he had the rugged look of an unfinished sculpture. Well over six feet tall, his broad shoulders, chiseled features, and solid stance gave him the appearance of a seasoned boxer. He wore black and white evening attire, stark colors that would make most men of her acquaintance appear sallow, but on him emphasized his masculinity.

He was a dark figure of a man, big and powerful, and his face had a confidence that bordered on arrogance. He certainly was not the kind of man a lady would want to be caught alone with on a ballroom terrace. On the few occasions they had spoken in the past, they had never gotten along.

She stiffened. "I don't know what you mean, Mr. Ramsey."

His eyes sharpened. "Ah, you remember me, Jane."

Jane. Not Lady Stanwell. His complete disregard of social decorum was one of the reasons he'd unnerved her.

"I was nearby and overheard those women. I watched you flee the ballroom," he said.

"I didn't *flee*," she blurted out, then bit her lip as she realized she had revealed too much.

He knew about her, of course. Everyone knew. She was highly conscious of his scrutiny. Mercifully, the moonlight hid the extent of her discomfort.

He took another step forward. "You shouldn't care."

"I don't," she said sharply.

He arched a dark eyebrow. "Then why are you hiding?"

"I'm *not*," she snapped.

Jane glanced back into the ballroom, wanting to run again. But this time from Gareth Ramsey's overbearing presence.

The orchestra began a waltz and the strains of the music drifted onto the terrace. Jane glanced into the ballroom. Olivia was dancing with Edward, and the young couple twirled across the parquet floor. Their faces were flushed with happiness, anticipating their wedding day and marriage with gleeful ignorance.

*Oh, to be so innocent.*

Mr. Ramsey chuckled and Jane raised her eyes to find him studying her. A corner of his full lips turned upward in a mocking expression, and she felt a strange pull low in her stomach.

For a fleeting instant, she imagined what kind of lover he would be.

Dark, dangerous, all consuming.

*Never!*

He may be the most masculine man she knew, but he was too intense, and instinct told her that he was not a man to be trifled with. A woman could easily lose control of an affair with Gareth Ramsey.

And that wasn't at all what she wanted.

She'd be far better off with the Simon Marburys of the *ton.*

Gareth took a step closer and Jane was suddenly nervous. She could smell his cologne, sandalwood and bergamot, and feel his black eyes taking in her features.

"I must return," Jane said.

"Why so soon after your mad flight?"

She refused to allow him to bait her. "There is to be a champagne toast to the future happiness of the engaged couple."

"Ah, and you are eager to participate?" he asked, noting her interest on the dance floor.

She shrugged. "Yes, of course. They are fortunate to have found true love."

Gareth scoffed. "Come now, my lady. Only fools believe in true love."

Her gaze narrowed. "Are you calling me a fool?"

"It depends," he drawled.

Jane had come to the same conclusion regarding affairs of the heart after Charles's suicide. But something about Gareth Ramsey's rudeness and dark scowl irked her. She had an overwhelming urge to argue with the intimidating man.

"Are you saying His Grace doesn't love Lady Olivia?" she asked.

"I know the duke. I'm not questioning his motives." Jane couldn't recall the last time she had felt anger toward someone other than herself or Charles. The feelings of vulnerability and dismay that had encompassed her moments ago as she hid behind the potted palm dissipated like a puff of smoke. In its place was a simmering fury.

"You think Lady Olivia is manipulating her betrothed?" she asked.

"It has crossed my mind. Westmont is a duke, and the lady has much more to gain from the match."

"Then your mind is demented," Jane snapped. She had never met such a maddening man in her entire life. Charles had been charming and handsome; Gareth Ramsey was like a bear. "You're wrong about Lady Olivia," Jane argued. "She is my closest friend, and she is an innocent young lady who has never been married."

"Where females are concerned, I believe age and experience have nothing to do with their ability to manipulate men to do their bidding. They are born with the knowledge."

She cocked her head to the side and narrowed her eyes. "What happened to turn you into such a bitter man, Mr. Ramsey? Did a woman break your heart? Or leave you at the altar?"

He laughed. "Hardly such nonsense. I would recover from such a trifle mishap. No, Lady Stanwell. As a barrister, my practice has opened my eyes."

"Pray tell me, sir, what type of legal practice could possibly result in your backward beliefs?"

"I dispose of unwanted wives."

Whatever answer she had expected, it wasn't *that*.

She'd known of his chosen profession, of course. All of London knew. Gareth Ramsey had obtained the near impossible—the coveted divorce for an influential viscount. News of the wife's torrid adulterous affairs—which had led to the Act of Parliament—had been in the newspapers for months afterwards. But Jane had forgotten about Mr. Ramsey's reputation and she could only surmise her faulty memory was due to the stress of tonight's events combined with his intimidating presence.

Gareth chuckled. "You are quite fascinating, Jane. It's good you're widowed."

She gasped. A gentleman would never dare say such a thing to a lady. Especially to a woman with her past.

She raised her chin a notch. "Why is that?"

He stepped close and leaned down to whisper in her ear. "Because if you were my wife, I wouldn't allow you to speak to a man alone on a ballroom terrace for any extended period of time."

She experienced a spark of excitement at his barbaric and possessive words and his warm breath against her cheek. A tingle of awareness ran down her spine, and her heart gave an involuntary jolt. Looking up, she met those dark eyes without flinching.

"Would you care to dance?" he asked.

"After voicing such harsh opinions, you are asking me to dance?" she asked incredulously.

"Yes."

"No."

"Why?" he demanded.

Jane measured him with a cool appraising look. "Because you are too cocksure, too arrogant, and far too jaded for me, Mr. Ramsey."

To her surprise, he burst out laughing.

She whirled and walked away. His deep chuckle followed her, the sound rippling down her spine.

It wasn't until she was back in the ballroom, passing the gossips who'd sent her fleeing onto the terrace, that she realized she was now too preoccupied with thoughts of Gareth Ramsey to care about the women's furtive glances and hushed whispers.

# Chapter Two

Gareth Ramsey walked into Turner's coffeehouse in the Strand and spotted his friends, Daniel Forster and Robert Ware, seated at a corner table. The strong aroma of coffee wafted through the room. "Well, what do you have for me?" Gareth said.

Daniel looked up and frowned. "Why do you assume I have anything?"

"Why meet in a coffeehouse this late in the afternoon? You usually prefer whiskey at White's," Gareth said.

When Daniel scowled and Robert chuckled, Gareth grinned. The three men had been close friends since attending Eton together. Daniel was the oldest son and heir to Viscount Clayborne. Robert Ware, otherwise known as Lord Kirkland, had inherited an earldom and recently married.

A waiter arrived and set down three steaming cups of coffee.

Gareth eyed his friends over the rim of his cup. "It's been a while since I've been contacted by the Home Office."

Robert had been first to be recruited as a safecracker. Thereafter, the government had need of gentlemen with access to Society, and Daniel and Gareth had been recruited.

After the death of the previous secretary, who had been found guilty of treason, the Home Office had been in turmoil. But times had changed, and Daniel had recently been appointed undersecretary and had influence over delegating certain espionage assignments for the Crown.

It had been close to a year since Gareth's last mission, which had resulted in the arrest of a corrupt Old Bailey judge who had accepted bribes in exchange for favorable verdicts. After his mission, Gareth had been busy with his own legal practice. But lately he'd experienced an unusual restlessness. He'd spent too many hours in his Gray's Inn chambers researching case law and counseling his disgruntled clients. A new mission was what he needed, and with Daniel's position as undersecretary, perhaps Gareth's time had come.

Daniel leaned across the table. "You were right. I do have something for you. Something that requires a gentleman of the *ton*."

Gareth grimaced. "I rarely associate with members of the *ton* unless they seek my services." Gareth avoided attending most of society's balls and events, and it was only when it aided his role as an agent that he accepted any invitations.

"You were at Newbury's ball last night," Robert pointed out.

Gareth shifted against the booth's unpadded back. "Lady Newbury is my mother's friend. I attended out of obligation."

Gareth didn't regret attending, but he'd never admit it to his friends. An image of Jane flashed through his mind — sleek blond hair, mysterious brown eyes, and an abundance of curves beneath her deep purple gown.

He knew about her past. The newspapers and scandal sheets had wasted vats of ink printing the gruesome news. Her husband had killed himself supposedly over a gaming debt. She was a widow, yes, but a black cloud hovered above her head from what the gentlemen at White's said. Lord Stanwell had been an addicted gambler of race horses and when his prized stallion had lost, he'd shot himself in the head.

Stupid bastard to leave her. And over a horse.

Gareth couldn't comprehend suicide over a woman, let alone a four-legged beast.

Whatever addiction the husband had suffered from, it was clear that his beautiful, young widow was left to pay the price.

From his vantage point on the terrace, Gareth had overheard the gossips at the refreshment table and witnessed Jane's flight. Something about her distress had tugged at him. A gentleman would have pitied her and offered her comfort, but he was no gentleman and he instinctively knew pity was not what Jane needed.

What he hadn't expected was the jolt of lust he'd felt when fury had flashed in her beautiful eyes and she'd refused him a dance.

Passion lay beneath the lady's cool surface.

Fascinating.

"The Home Office suspects corruption from one of its military suppliers," Daniel spoke, drawing Gareth's attention back to his friends.

Gareth took a sip of coffee before lowering his cup. "A military supplier? Don't tell me we're talking about a trivial matter such as boots that fall apart?"

"It's much more serious than that," Daniel said. "Generals have reported faulty cannons on the battlefield. Cannons that cannot withstand the heat and fail after several uses with disastrous results. They explode and wound or kill our own men."

"Several companies manufacture cannons. Can you identify which one?" Gareth said.

"Yes, but it was tricky," Daniel said. "Not all the cannons were inferior, less than a quarter of the production. The involved parties were clever, you see. They also bribed military inspectors when the cannons were tested. It was a combination of corruption and collusion. But we have identified the maker of the inferior cannons."

"Who?" Gareth asked.

"The Marbury Company," Daniel said.

"The old man? Hasn't he been in business for years?" Even Gareth had heard of Sir Vincent Marbury. Well into his seventies, he was an avid supporter of Wellington and had been knighted for his efforts in supplying the Crown's troops.

Daniel cleared his throat. "It's true. Sir Vincent Marbury received a royal charter to incorporate the Marbury Company in 1795. Thereafter, the Board of Ordnance granted him a contract to supply cannons to the army. But he's been ill and bedridden for some time. His son is running the business."

Gareth scoffed. "Simon Marbury? You think that dandy is behind this scheme?"

"We are almost certain," Daniel said.

"Then arrest him. Why involve me?" Gareth said.

Daniel set down his cup. "We know he is the mastermind, but we don't know how many others are involved. Which military inspectors? Which officers? We need an agent to follow Simon Marbury and unearth this information."

Gareth's brows drew downward. "I'm just to shadow him?"

Robert spoke up. "Don't sound so sour. I've had plenty of missions where I've had to follow a man around for months."

Gareth glared at Robert. "Then you take it."

"I'm retired from active duty, remember?" Robert said.

Gareth scowled. Since Robert had married Lady Sophia, he no longer took on missions, but acted as an advisor to the Home Office and was therefore privy to the conversation.

"You're both wrong in this instance," Daniel said. "Gareth isn't just to watch Simon Marbury, but to befriend him and convince him to do business with you. Your legal background combined with your access to society makes you the perfect candidate for this."

"I see."

Daniel cleared his throat. "It's an important mission. The Crown does not want the truth behind the faulty cannons in the newspapers. This must be handled discreetly."

"All right," Gareth agreed. He wanted to get back to work for the Home Office, and if this was the only mission available, he would accept it.

Daniel cleared his throat again. "As the Season is just beginning, you should have no trouble watching Simon Marbury. He's quite the town tulip, and I'm told he attends many events."

Gareth hated the Season and the thought of attending endless rounds of tedious attractions left a sourness in the pit of his stomach. "Splendid."

An unbidden thought came to mind. If more balls and parties were requisite to his assignment, he would likely run into Lady Stanwell. He'd purposely manipulated Jane at the ball by using his reputation to rile her temper. He'd wanted to distract her from the malicious gossip of the magpies, and it had worked.

He knew his profession unnerved society ladies. It didn't matter that he'd stumbled upon what had now become his specialty area of legal practice. The fact was, he'd handled a solitary case for Viscount Harrison, and by proving his wife's adultery, had obtained the man a divorce through an Act of Parliament. Word had immediately spread, and wealthy and titled men had flocked to his Gray's Inn chambers. Somehow he'd ended up taking on more and more clients. He promised them nothing, charged his fees, and often obtained for them the more readily available remedies of legal separation or monetary damages for criminal conversation.

He could still feel the lust reverberating through his body at the spark of fury in Jane's eyes after he'd insulted her friend. It had been a long time since he'd been challenged— in or out of the bedroom.

*Christ.* What was he thinking? He had a job to do and he couldn't afford any distractions.

Jane may be enticing, but she was a lady—far from his type. He preferred courtesans and mistresses. Not sensitive, emotionally damaged widows. He needed to forget her and her troubles.

"I can think of no better man for the mission," Daniel said.

Gareth nodded. "Don't worry. I'll befriend Simon Marbury. It won't take me long to learn all his sordid secrets."

• • •

"Simon Marbury is perfect," Jane announced.

"He is very attractive," Olivia said.

Olivia sat on the bench seat at the end of the bed and smoothed her skirts. The two were in Jane's bedchamber looking over her wardrobe. Too many dresses were black — black crepe, black bombazine silk, and black wool.

Last night's purple gown stood out like a beacon of hope.

Jane was convinced of her plans. It was time for a completely different experience from her sheltered childhood and her disappointing marriage.

All her life, decisions had been made for her. First by her family when they arranged her marriage, then by her husband.

Now she would make her own choices. Starting with her future lover.

"Are you certain about Mr. Marbury?" Olivia asked.

Jane recalled Simon Marbury's attractive features — his golden hair, blue eyes, and slight build. She knew little else about him, but she was confident she could approach him at the next event. From what she'd heard, he rarely declined an invitation during the Season.

The image in her mind changed and a picture of Gareth Ramsey arose. Marbury's fair looks were in stark contrast to the sinfully dark, broad-shouldered Mr. Ramsey.

Jane turned back to Olivia. "I'm fairly certain about Simon Marbury, but I've decided to comprise a list of others just in case."

"A list?" Olivia said.

"Why not?" Jane said defensively. "After years of marriage to a selfish husband who never truly loved me, I'm entitled to some pleasure."

"O-of course," Olivia stammered. "I didn't mean to suggest otherwise. Do you have someone in mind?"

"I want a man who looks at me with passion and desire."

"Didn't Charles ever—"

"No, Charles never looked at me that way." She may have thought so at first, but Charles had been an addicted gambler and well-practiced at lying.

And she had been so young and naive.

"Other than Mr. Marbury, who else do you have in mind?" Olivia asked.

"I've made a list of eligible candidates in London." Jane handed Olivia the piece of foolscap she had been working on.

Olivia unfolded the paper and read aloud the header at the top of the page. "*Possible Candidates as Lovers.*"

Olivia scanned the page before looking up. "The men listed here are all dandies and members of the *ton.*"

"I've selected men who won't quibble about having a private affair with the widow of the Earl of Stanwell," Jane said. "Since I have no desire to marry again, intelligence is not an important factor. I prefer to be in control, the cleverer partner. I seek only a skilled lover in the bedroom, not a conversationalist."

Olivia lowered the paper. "I'm shocked. Not because you desire a lover—I think you deserve happiness after all you've been through—but because there is no trace of the grieving, withdrawn widow I've grown accustomed to."

Jane knew it was true. The emotions that had afflicted her after Charles's suicide and the abrupt end of their three-year marriage had been tumultuous. She'd suffered bouts of melancholy for days followed by fits of rage. Not one unbroken mirror remained in her house.

But now, finally, she was finished shedding tears over

love lost and tragedy.

It really hadn't been love anyway, had it?

She had loved; her husband had not.

It was time to put the past behind her and move on. Time to live, time to enjoy life…perhaps time to open her heart to another?

No, never that. But that didn't mean she couldn't enjoy male companionship, even a lusty bed partner. Sex did not have to be associated with love. Charles had shared her bed without giving her his heart, hadn't he? She could write a long list of the married and widowed women of the *beau monde* who engaged in scandalous affairs.

Why not her?

"Aren't you fearful of pregnancy?" Olivia asked.

Jane stopped short as a heaviness centered in her chest. "My greatest regret is that I was unable to conceive during my marriage. A doctor declared me barren."

"I'm so sorry, Jane."

Jane pushed aside her dismay. "It matters naught now. You see, there's no risk of pregnancy if I take a lover." She took a deep breath. "You are my closest friend, Olivia, and your opinion matters to me. Do you completely disapprove?"

A mischievous smile touched Olivia's lips. "No, I do not disapprove. Let's go through your list then, shall we?" She held up the paper and read the first name aloud. "The Earl of Townsend."

"Do you think he's too old? He's been widowed for five years now and close to fifty," Jane said.

"His dress is always meticulous and he spends a considerable amount of time with his tailor. What makes you think he's looking for a lover?" Olivia asked.

"You think him too effeminate?" Jane asked.

"It has struck my mind."

"Keep going."

Olivia read the next name. "The Marquess of Carr." She looked at Jane. "He's an incorrigible rake. Lady Rumpole claims that he speaks freely of his affairs and enjoys being the center of attention."

"That won't do," Jane said, shaking her head. "I prefer discretion. What about Sir Walter Miller?"

Olivia wrinkled her nose. "He's a notorious fortune hunter and must marry for money. He's courting Alice Hitchens whose father has made a huge sum in shipping."

"Then he'd be a fool to start an affair. It could ruin his chances of a wealthy union. How about Baron Umbridge?" Jane asked.

A look of unease crossed Olivia's face. "He gambles. He once borrowed money from Father. The loan was never repaid."

Jane's jaw stiffened. "I'd rather bed a leper than another gambler." She held out her hand.

Olivia gave the list back to Jane, who marched to the escritoire, dipped the quill in ink, and proceeded to cross off Baron Umbridge's name with a long black line.

"Perhaps there is a man who is not on your list that would… fulfill your requirements and accommodate you," Olivia said.

Jane set the quill down. Once again, an unbidden image of another man came to mind. Black eyes and a cynical twist to hard lips. Not handsome like Charles, but a towering dominant male with a muscular frame.

She tried to banish the thought. The last man she should be thinking of was Gareth Ramsey.

He was rude, obstinate, insulting—unlike her charming

late husband in every way. Perhaps that's what made Mr. Ramsey even slightly attractive.

Still, she couldn't help but wonder if he had thought of her since he had asked her to dance at last night's ball.

"I shall think of additional names." Jane quickly lowered her gaze before Olivia could read her thoughts.

"Meanwhile it shouldn't be difficult to cross paths with Mr. Marbury. He has a reputation for enjoying all the Season has to offer. Mother aided Lady Sefton with the guest list for her upcoming annual masquerade and Simon Marbury was included."

Jane looked up and smiled. "I received an invitation as well. I do believe I'll accept."

# Chapter Three

The evening of Lady Sefton's ball arrived a week later. In a daring move Jane chose to dress in a scarlet gown. She had ordered the deep silk from the most fashionable London modiste, and the bodice was cut to show a provocative amount of cleavage and hug her curves.

"You look lovely, Jane."

Jane smoothed her skirts and turned to see her maternal aunt in the doorway. Aunt Eleanor was a plump elderly woman with a steel gray bun. Her arthritic joints occasionally pained her, so she was never without her cane. Jane had moved into her town home in Piccadilly soon after Charles died. Eleanor was a dear mother-like figure to her, and as affectionate as her own birth mother had been before her death.

Again Jane was grateful for her widow's portion, which Charles had been unable to gamble away. Combined with her aunt's wealth, the two women had been able to keep their staff and maintain a comfortable standard of living.

"You do not think the scarlet is too daring?" Jane asked.

Eleanor clicked her tongue. "Nonsense. You are a beautiful woman who should wear beautiful clothes. Now sit and let Monique style your hair."

Jane obediently sat at her dressing table as her maid's skilled fingers fashioned her blond hair into stylish curls atop her head. Monique purposely left a loose tendril to brush her cheek and rest against the swell of her breast. Jane barely recognized herself as she gazed into the looking glass.

Aunt Eleanor sighed. "All the men will be drawn to you."

Jane wrinkled her nose. "I highly doubt it. My reputation, remember?"

"Posh! You have been hiding behind ugly black gowns. Just wait until they see you tonight."

Jane stood and kissed her aunt's wrinkled cheek. "I wish you could come." Her aunt rarely left the comfort of her home.

Eleanor stomped her cane. "Nonsense. I'm an old lady and I've attended my fair share of balls." She handed Jane a bejeweled scarlet half-mask. "Now you'd best hurry, my dear. The carriage is waiting."

A short ride later, Jane stepped into the Lady Sefton's ballroom with a purpose. Since it was a masquerade, the guests were not announced by a majordomo and a frisson of mystery and excitement pervaded the room.

Jane adjusted her half-mask and took a glass of champagne from a liveried servant's tray. She scanned the room and spotted Olivia by the dance floor talking to a group of women. Olivia was stunning in a pink satin gown with a spangled mask. She looked up, met Jane's eyes, and smiled. Even masked, they easily recognized each other.

Olivia excused herself from the women, then walked over to Jane. Olivia's gaze traveled over the scarlet gown. "You look so different."

"It's the dress," Jane said.

Olivia tilted her head to the side and regarded her. "No. It's not just the dress. It's *you*. And it's about time, if I dare say so."

Male laughter drew Jane's attention to where Simon Marbury stood with a group of friends, his slim mask doing little to hide his identity. She also recognized one of the other young men as Lord Curran, Olivia's cousin.

"Marbury is here," Olivia whispered.

Jane swallowed. "How can I gain an introduction?"

Olivia shook her head. "I don't think there's a need. He's coming over to us."

Simon approached, accompanied by Lord Curran.

Simon's male perfection completely overshadowed Curran. Simon wore his fair hair *à la Brutus*, a style currently popular with the dandies of the *ton*. His meticulously tailored double-breasted coat was embellished with large gold buttons, and his snowy cravat was intricately folded. Even partially obscured by the mask, his features were so flawless, so symmetrical, that any more delicacy would have made him too beautiful for a man.

"Good evening, ladies," Lord Curran said.

Jane and Olivia curtsied.

"Allow me to introduce an admirer, Mr. Simon Marbury," said Lord Curran.

Simon bowed. "Hello, Lady Olivia. Your cousin already revealed your identity to me." He then turned his attention to Jane. His eyes roved over the scarlet gown and lingered on the fat ruby necklace resting between her cleavage. "And who is this lovely lady in disguise?"

Jane felt a thrill of excitement and her confidence spiraled upward.

"Why, Mr. Marbury. Surely you understand tonight is a masquerade. Even though Lord Curran pointed me out to you," Olivia said, shooting her cousin a disapproving glare, "I insist on keeping my friend's identity secret."

Jane smiled coyly. "At least until after midnight, Mr. Marbury."

Sapphire eyes shone from behind Simon's slim mask. "You have an unfair advantage, my lady, as you already know my name."

"I have heard much about you," Jane said, emboldened by his interest.

He arched a brow. "Oh?"

"You are an excellent dancer."

"I must live up to my reputation. May I have the next dance?"

"I'm afraid my dance card is full until after the supper hour, sir," Jane said.

"I refused to be dissuaded. You must promise to save a waltz for me," Simon insisted.

Olivia waited until Simon departed with Lord Curran before turning to Jane. "Clever to refuse him a dance."

"I didn't refuse him. I just made him wait until later in the evening," Jane said.

"From the way he looked at you, he'll be sure to return to claim the waltz." Olivia clasped Jane's hand. "Come. Let's dance with my brothers and make a good show for Mr. Marbury."

Jane let Olivia lead her away. Out of the corner of her eye, she spotted a tall figure step through the open doors leading onto the terrace. She turned to get a better look, but whoever she'd thought she'd seen was gone. Was Gareth Ramsey in attendance tonight? Her heartbeat quickened, and she pressed a hand to her chest and took a deep breath. She was reacting foolishly. It could have been any tall gentleman guest. Why did Gareth have to immediately intrude into her thoughts?

An even more disturbing thought sprang to mind: did she *want* him to be here?

• • •

Jane peered into the library to ensure it was vacant before entering. Her list had been calling out to her all evening and she needed a secluded room to think.

Her plan was working. Simon Marbury wanted to dance with her. Others had expressed interest as well. Once a man of Simon's status had deemed her worthy of attention, others had come forward.

The scarlet gown had worked wonders.

Or was it her newfound confidence and determination?

Either way, she was one step closer to finding a lover. She should be happy that her well-laid plans were working.

Yet something was missing.

Opening her reticule, she removed the list. A large oak desk sat in front of a bay window flanked on both sides by tall, mahogany bookshelves. She removed her mask and gloves and placed them on the desk. The casement was cracked open a few inches, allowing a cool, evening breeze to blow in. A lantern in the corner of the desk illuminated the polished wood grain.

One unwritten name haunted her.

She reached for a quill on the desk, dipped it in an inkwell, and wrote Gareth Ramsey's initials at the bottom of the list. She had originally wanted to put his name at the top, but she had held back. She didn't want to show it to Olivia.

If Olivia deciphered the initials and figured out who Jane meant, it would raise unwanted questions that she was not prepared to answer.

Gareth was a bachelor who oozed virility, but he didn't possess the qualities that she'd set forth. He was too intelligent and too dominant. Olivia would surely point out these flaws.

Jane stood and stared out the window at the full moon. A slight breeze from the open window ruffled the curtains, then blew the list beneath the nearby bookshelf.

"Oh!" Jane crouched down by the bookshelf and reached beneath the scalloped edge. Her fingers just grazed the foolscap. Curls loosened from her coiffure. Pushing the blond strands back with an impatient hand, she stretched further and further until…

"Got you!" The tips of two fingers grasped the edge and pulled it out.

"Well, well. I hadn't expected such a magnificent view upon my arrival."

Jane whirled around at the deep voice to find Gareth Ramsey standing in the open doorway. Striding forward, he stood over her — a tall, broad, and muscular man.

She sat back on her heels, looking up at him in shock. "You!"

"Yes. Me." He extended a large hand.

Her eyes traveled from his outstretched hand to his face and back again. He was unmasked and just as she remembered — rugged features, sardonic black eyes, curling jet hair, and full lips that always seemed to curve at the corners in a mocking smile.

He quirked an eyebrow questioningly. "Are you going to take my hand or gape up at me all evening?"

She came to her senses and placed her hand in his. His palm was big and callused. He pulled her to her feet as if she weighed no more than thistledown, and a shiver of awareness crept down her spine.

She frowned. "You shouldn't sneak up on someone. It's not polite."

A flash of humor lit his eyes. "I wasn't the one sneaking." He glanced at the list in her fist. "What are you up to?"

She held the paper behind her back. "What are you doing here?"

He arched a dark eyebrow. "I was invited."

What a silly question. Of course he was invited. A gentleman didn't just show up at a masquerade without being welcomed by the host.

"I see."

Disappointment pierced her. What had she expected? That he was in attendance tonight just to see her?

*Ridiculous.*

She really needed to get a hold of her rioting emotions. The last time she had met him, she'd lost her temper. It appeared she had done so again. What was it about the man that was so infuriating?

"If you'll excuse me, I'll just be on my way." She attempted to brush past him lest he see something in her face that she did not want revealed.

He didn't budge. "No."

"No?"

"Not until you tell me what you've stolen."

"Stolen?"

"Something from the earl's desk."

Her jaw dropped. "How dare you!"

"Daring has nothing to do with it." Reaching behind her, he plucked the list out of her hand so fast she had no time to react.

"Give that back!"

He held the list up high. He was extremely tall and she had no hope of reaching it. Still, she jumped and tried. "You arrogant swine!"

She jumped twice more and the remaining curls tumbled from her coiffure across her shoulders and down her back.

His eyes darkened as he looked down at her. "If I had any doubt before that this was important, I don't now. I must see for myself."

To her horror, he unfolded the paper and read aloud. "Possible Candidates as Lovers." For a brief instant his face hardened, then the cool, confident mask descended once again.

"Are you serious?" he asked, mockingly.

Never had she been so embarrassed in her life. Not even when she'd tripped after being announced at Lady Tavistock's ball as a first year debutante.

But then her humiliation veered into anger. How dare he rip a private document from her hand and then mock her?

She placed her hands on her hips and lifted her chin. "I am quite serious. I've decided to turn over a new leaf."

He cocked an eyebrow. "Turn over a new leaf?"

"Yes."

He glanced at the list and smirked. "The Marquess of Carr, Sir Miller, Baron Umbridge, and the Earl of Townsend?"

"What's wrong with them?"

"Carr is an idiot, Miller is an avaricious fortune hunter, Umbridge will bet on anything and is in debt up to his neck, and Townsend was thrilled at his wife's passing."

"That's a falsehood about Townsend. He's publically grieving and still wears black two years later."

Gareth rolled his eyes. "The Earl of Townsend is a hypocrite. He sought out my services when his wife was alive. He called her a witch and wanted her gone."

She gasped.

Ignoring her dismay, his eyes narrowed slightly. "Mr. Simon Marbury is also on your list."

She met his stare. "You cannot possibly criticize the man."

Something flickered in his eyes, something dark and unpleasant. "Stay away from him."

"You cannot tell me what to do."

"The man is a dissolute pleasure seeker."

"Half of the gentlemen of my acquaintance match that description."

"Your behavior is reckless."

Her anger rose a notch. "There's nothing reckless about my list. To the contrary, it's very well planned."

He looked back at the paper and smiled arrogantly. "If you refuse to come to your senses, then I have just one question for you."

"What?"

"Why am I last on your list?"

She wanted to laugh at that. He would have been first, had she dared. "It's not you," she lied. Thank heavens she hadn't written out his full name.

"I don't believe you," he said. "It clearly has my initials."

She placed her hands on her hips. "That could stand for

anyone."

"I'm well versed at reading people. You're a bad liar."

"You're a conceited fool."

His eyes narrowed and for a heartbeat she thought she had gone too far, but then he threw back his head and laughed.

"You are a handful, Jane. You need a man to keep you in line. A man that can teach you passion, not these fools." With deliberate movements, he folded the list and slipped it into the inside pocket of his jacket. "I do believe I'll keep this."

Reason fled. She threw herself at him, fully intending to strike him and take the list back with physical force. But as she lunged forward, her heel snagged in the thick carpet. She stumbled, lost her balance, and fell headlong into his solid chest.

He grunted as she took him by surprise. Strong arms grasped around her waist as they tumbled onto the settee, Jane sprawled on top of him.

"Oh!"

She was aware of every hard inch of him. He was completely unlike Charles or any of the popinjays she had put on her list. He was all male—big, hard, and dangerous. His mouth was mere inches from hers.

"You needn't have worked yourself up into such a fury, although I must admit I don't mind. I intended to give the list back to you. I was jesting," he said.

His eyes weren't black, but deep coffee-brown. His lips full and sensual.

"Oh. I see." She made no attempt to rise, and he made no effort to assist her to her feet.

"But I am serious about the character of the men on your list. None of them are appropriate for the position, especially Marbury."

"And you know others who are?"

"Other. And yes." His eyes raked her face with a sensuality that was unmistakable. She started to rise, but his arms tightened about her, forcing her to remain pressed against him.

"Then you truly are a fool, Mr. Ramsey. You are the last person I'd want as a lov—"

He captured her lips in a searing kiss. Drawing her tightly to him, her breasts were crushed against his solid chest. The heat emanated from his body and seeped into hers, flooding her limbs with languid passion. His lips, which had appeared carved of marble, were not cold, hard, or demanding as she had initially thought, but sinfully seductive. He explored her mouth with tantalizing persuasiveness, and coaxed her response like one would stoke a slow burning fire.

Her eyelids fluttered closed. She grasped his forearms to steady herself, then slid her hands up his arms. His biceps were enormous, rock hard and pulsing with heat. His size should have alarmed her; Charles had been young, but his love of drink and gambling had turned him soft. Simon Marbury appeared well built, but she suspected his tailor had added padding to his coat to increase the breadth of his shoulders.

Nothing about Gareth Ramsey was padded or soft. The shock of his muscular frame ran through her body. But instead of fear, his strength and power thrilled her.

He licked her bottom lip and sucked the delicate fullness into his mouth like he was savoring a ripe plumb. The simmering heat in her veins turning scalding hot. The contrast of their sizes and his tightly leashed lust was a potent aphrodisiac. She'd never experienced it before.

Certainly not with Charles.

Gareth's intense sexuality excited her, and she wanted to be ravaged by him—to know what it felt like to be fiercely desired by a man.

She stopped herself just in time. This wasn't a man she could control. The passion that inched through her veins was as dangerous as it was thrilling, and without a doubt she knew that she wouldn't be able to have a casual affair with Gareth Ramsey.

No. She wanted a lover without complications. A man who would not hurt her.

With Gareth Ramsey she would get scorched.

She pushed against his solid chest. Her efforts were in vain. He let her place inches between them, rather than allow her to rise.

"Release me. This is wrong."

The smoldering flame she saw in his eyes startled her.

"It's perfect. Neither of us wants to marry, and you are in search of a candidate. Let me be your lover."

"Never!"

"We shall see."

She pressed harder against his chest. "Let me up."

"As you wish, my lady."

He released her and handed her the list. "This is a very bad idea."

She ignored him and snatched the paper from his hand. Rising as gracefully as possible on shaky legs, she smoothed her rumpled skirts with damp palms and glared at him. "It's best if we avoid each other from now on."

He stood and looked down at her intently. "As the Season has started, that will prove difficult."

"I suggest you try your best," she said, "As I shall do!" Then she spun on her heel, snatched her discarded gloves and mask from the desk, and marched from the room.

# Chapter Four

Jane's heart raced as she fled the library. She halted in a dim alcove to straighten her disheveled hair with her fingers, tie her half mask back in place, and slip on her gloves. If she had a mirror, she knew her cheeks would be flushed. Silently counting to ten, she tried desperately to calm her breathing before returning to the ballroom.

Olivia approached as soon as Jane stepped into the room.

"Where were you? You missed the supper room," Olivia said.

"I needed some time to think and found myself in Lady Sefton's library," Jane said.

Olivia surveyed her kindly. "You're pink. Are you feeling well?"

"I'm fine, truly. I just needed some time alone." She should tell Olivia truth, but she couldn't bring herself to admit what had transpired between herself and Gareth Ramsey. Goodness, she couldn't even comprehend it herself. She didn't know which was more shocking, his kiss or her own eager response.

The crowd was making its way back into the ballroom. The musicians began tuning their instruments.

"Mr. Marbury approaches. You promised him a waltz, remember?"

Had she? It seemed like such a long time had passed since she'd spoken with Simon.

Her kiss with Gareth Ramsey was too fresh in her mind. A vivid image of his lips claiming hers, of him crushing her to his hard chest, sent the pit of her stomach into a wild swirl. Perhaps it was convenient she had been sprawled across his big body on the settee since her knees had instantly weakened. Surely she would have fallen when his tongue traced the soft fullness of her lips. His kiss had been as challenging as it was tantalizing and left her feeling a burning desire, an aching need, for more.

*Sweet lord.*

The orchestra struck up a waltz.

Simon came forward and bowed. "Dear mystery lady, I do believe you promised me this dance."

She blinked and managed a tremulous smile. This was what she wanted. The reason she'd attended tonight's masquerade and worn the daring scarlet gown. Jane took a quick breath and pushed Mr. Ramsey out of her thoughts. She couldn't— *wouldn't*—allow the arrogant man to derail her well-laid plans.

Jane placed a gloved hand on Simon's sleeve, and he led her to the dance floor and swept her into the music.

Jane's feet moved of their own accord across the polished floor. The colorful gowns of the guests whirled by as they danced, and she glanced up at her partner. Simon was even more strikingly handsome up close with his fair hair, patrician features, and blue eyes. He smiled, revealing straight, white teeth.

He was polished. Cool. A rogue through and through.

Perfect for her purposes.

Yet a frisson of unease pierced her spine. She may not be a virgin, but she was far from an experienced courtesan. She needed a man to teach her. Could he be the one?

Or was he interested only in his pleasure?

*Just like Charles had been.*

She couldn't judge Simon Marbury yet; she hardly knew him. She couldn't trust what Gareth Ramsey had said about the man. She suspected Ramsey's pride was wounded because her list hadn't named him first. She wouldn't put it past him to say anything to slander Simon.

No, she wouldn't fall for that trap. She needed more time with Marbury to draw her own conclusions about his character.

Simon's smile widened. "Who are you? I must know. I wish to call upon you for a ride in Hyde Park."

She hesitated. He was clearly interested, but if she revealed her identity would he remain so?

"I shall meet you in the park. I prefer to keep tonight a mystery," she said.

"Why?"

"It adds to the excitement, don't you agree?"

His sapphire eyes glittered with eagerness. And something else. Something almost predatory.

Nonsense. He asked for spin around Hyde Park. Harmless to be sure. This was what she wanted, she reminded herself. He was the perfect candidate. The perfect choice.

His eyes roamed her face, and she knew he attempted

to see behind her mask. "How will I know it's you in the park?" he said.

"You'll know, Mr. Marbury."

"Simon. Call me Simon.

• • •

Simon Marbury was on Jane's list.

Bloody hell.

Gareth stayed in the library after Jane departed. He paced the thick Brussels carpet, deep in thought.

He'd believed the mission would be simple. Engage Marbury and learn his secrets. Only now, Jane added a complication and he didn't like complications. He pictured her bent over, reaching behind the desk. Layers of silk couldn't completely hide a curvaceous bottom that would tempt any man to touch her.

*Damn.*

His mission had new consequences. He'd been assigned to watch Marbury. Now he needed to keep an eye on Lady Stanwell.

Another image rose in his mind of her in the scarlet gown that accentuated the lush curves of her breasts. Her golden hair styled in loose curls that made a man want to remove the pins and feel all that silken hair in his hands. To feel the tresses trail down his chest and lower still…

What was wrong with him? He wasn't a randy schoolboy panting after his first girl. He was used to completely different types of women, skilled courtesans who placed no emotional demands on him.

Jane was not his type.

He clenched and unclenched his fists. Took a deep breath and exhaled slowly. Confident he had his thoughts and his body under control, Gareth withdrew his mask from his jacket pocket and headed back to the masquerade.

He stopped short in the entranceway.

Jane was dancing with Simon Marbury. Not just any dance, but the waltz. Simon held her close, hands at her waist. Her gloved hands rested on his shoulders as she gazed up at him. They were well partnered and glided effortlessly across the dance floor.

Gareth wasn't the only one to notice. Women watched with envious looks behind fluttering fans. Men stared at Jane in the form-hugging scarlet.

Possessiveness fired through Gareth's bloodstream with the force of a shot. He clamped his jaw tight.

Candlelight reflected off Jane's golden curls and the large ruby nestled in her ample cleavage. Simon leaned toward her and spoke, a watchful fixity in his face. Jane tilted her head to the side, exposing the long, graceful line of her neck, and laughed.

All thoughts of distancing himself from the lady fled. Jane wanted a lover and Simon Marbury was on her list. She was not only reckless, but foolish. Marbury wasn't just a criminal who sold substandard cannons to the military—his file spoke of seedy brothels and unusual sexual practices.

The importance of Gareth's mission ratcheted up a notch. He had a job to do, and he felt the urgency to finish it quickly.

• • •

At last the waltz ended, and Jane allowed Simon to escort her to the refreshment table. If the dance were any indication, they would be well suited partners. Yet Jane found herself scanning the ballroom for a tall, dark-haired man. She wasn't certain if it was out of trepidation or interest, but she needn't have worried.

Mr. Ramsey wasn't present.

Simon handed her a glass of lemonade. She took a sip and it tasted sickeningly sweet. She was just about to suggest he escort her onto the terrace for a breath of fresh air when a deep-timbered voice sounded behind her.

"Mr. Marbury."

Jane whirled to see Gareth Ramsey approach. Her heart skipped a beat. Where on earth had he come from? Her first instinct was to flee, but that would certainly raise unwanted questions. She forced herself to stand still beside Simon as she studied Gareth Ramsey beneath lowered lashes.

For such a large man, he moved with the grace and stealth of a panther. His rugged features held a certain sensuality, and even in the crowded ballroom, his presence was compelling.

But why would he seek Simon out?

Mr. Ramsey stopped before them, quite openly studying her. She flushed, grateful her mask covered part of her face. Unbidden images flashed through her mind. He wouldn't dare mention their encounter in the library, would he? An even more terrifying realization washed over her. He not only knew her identity, but he was aware of her secret list of potential lovers. Would he disclose her name and mention the list?

Simon looked at Gareth. "Are we acquainted?"

"I'm Gareth Ramsey and I met your father years ago. I've heard Sir Marbury is ill and wanted to pass along my well wishes to your mother."

"Thank you for your concern." Simon motioned to Jane. "I would introduce you, but the lady prefers to remain anonymous."

"There's no need for introductions." Gareth looked at Jane and grinned. "Good evening, Lady Stanwell. Are you enjoying the masquerade?"

A brief flicker of surprise crossed Simon's face, but it was swiftly masked with a polite smile.

Jane shot Gareth a deadly look only to find a smug grin on his face.

*He knew I wished to remain unknown!*

She stiffened, clutching the glass of lemonade so tightly she feared it would shatter. She knew it was the moment of truth. Her identity concerned Simon, but he must not reconsider his interest.

Acting quickly, she placed her hand on Simon's sleeve, looked up at him, and moistened her bottom lip.

Simon's gaze immediately dropped to her mouth.

"Oh, Mr. Marbury. I had thought to keep my identity a surprise," she said huskily.

A quick glance at Gareth revealed his grin had disappeared. A muscle flicked angrily at his jaw.

Jane felt a thrill of satisfaction.

"No matter, Lady Stanwell," Simon said.

Jane didn't know why Gareth had sought out Simon. She doubted he'd interrupted them for the sole reason of expressing his concern for Simon's ill father, and she suspected that Gareth had an ulterior motive. The urge to leave before he goaded her into saying something she'd regret was strong. She didn't trust him. More than that, she didn't trust herself around him. He had a way of riling her temper like none other.

Jane scanned the room and was relieved to see Olivia by the dance floor. She quickly curtsied. "If you gentlemen will please excuse me, I see a friend."

Simon bowed. "Of course."

Gareth's eyes bore into hers. He was mocking her, and he knew exactly why she was fleeing. Jane knew leaving was the best option, yet she struggled with the urge to stay and meet his gaze in challenge. *Don't be a fool!* Engaging him would not only be reckless, but dangerous.

• • •

Gareth waited until Jane departed before engaging Marbury. "I have other reasons to speak with you. Business reasons."

Simon looked at him curiously. "I recall hearing about you, Mr. Ramsey. You work as a barrister, correct?"

"Yes."

Simon laughed. "As I am a bachelor with no wife to dispose of, I have no need of your services."

"You misunderstand," Gareth said. "I have a client who wants to invest in your company."

"He should see my secretary."

"No. It must be kept quiet. He wants only to deal with you."

"I'm not looking for new investors at this—"

"Perhaps we can go elsewhere and discuss the details. I understand you like Satan's Lair."

Marbury's nostrils flared slightly. Gareth had done his research and knew the exclusive gambling hell on Bennett Street was one of Marbury's weaknesses.

"No harm in hearing out your friend's plans," Simon said. "I'm obligated to stay only an hour more at the masquerade. Let's meet later tonight."

...

Gareth wandered the ballroom, stopping only to talk to several acquaintances. Things were progressing as planned. Simon would meet him at the gambling club later tonight, and Gareth would reveal his "mysterious client's" offer to invest in the Marbury Company.

As far as Jane was concerned, he'd purposely sought out Marbury when he was with her. Gareth still couldn't believe that of all the men in attendance tonight, she had convinced herself that she wanted Simon.

Gareth scanned the ballroom until he spotted Jane speaking with a group of young women. He waited until the orchestra began the next song, a lively Scottish reel, and several of the ladies paired off with gentlemen.

He strode over to Jane and grasped her sleeve before anyone could ask her to dance.

She whirled around to stare up at him in astonishment. "What are you doing?"

"May I have a quick word with you on the terrace?"

"I told you we should avoid each other," she whispered vehemently.

His lips tugged in a smile. "I was never good at following instructions." The crowd was momentarily distracted as the dance began, and he quickly steered Jane toward the open French doors leading outside.

The terrace was empty. Clouds dimmed the light of a crescent moon, and torches cast light and shadows on the Roman statues in the manicured gardens below. The scene reminded him of the last time he had spoken to her on a terrace. The only difference then was that Jane had been distraught when she'd fled outside before, whereas now she simmered with fury.

She tilted her head back and glared at him. "What do you want?"

"I thought I made myself clear in the library." He couldn't help himself. She was truly lovely when she was angry. A cool evening breeze ruffled tendrils of hair at her nape. His fingers itched to reach out and touch the loose curl that rested against the swell of her breast above her bodice.

"Never speak of it again." She shot him a withering glance, then looked both ways to ensure they were truly alone on the terrace. "Now why did you seek out Mr. Marbury tonight?"

"I thought to offer support for his ill father."

"Don't be ridiculous. You could have done that at any time. You chose to purposely interfere when I was enjoying a pleasant conversation with him."

"A pleasant conversation? Is that all you were enjoying?"

"It's none of your concern," she snapped.

She was right. It wasn't his business who she picked for her next lover. But he didn't like it. "Be careful, my lady. You play with fire."

"Your attempts to dissuade me won't work. I know your game. You thought by revealing my identity to Mr. Marbury he would lose interest in me. After all, what man would choose to spend time with the damaged widow who drove her husband to harm himself?"

For a brief instant her voice wavered and a flash of pain lit her eyes, but she recovered quickly. Still, her distress was enough to make him want to pull her into his arms and kiss her senseless, until she knew exactly what type of man wanted her.

She must have sensed his thoughts, for her eyes narrowed and her back straightened. The fire was back in her eyes.

"You failed, Mr. Ramsey. It didn't work."

Here was his chance. He needed to find out Marbury's whereabouts. His mission required that he learn as much about the man as possible, then use it to his advantage. Nothing could be overlooked. Using others to unearth information came naturally to Gareth. He felt no guilt.

Yet a deeper part of him also wanted to know if Jane was spending time with Marbury. He didn't know why. Only that it bothered him, damn it.

"Oh? Does Marbury want to see you again? To come calling at your home?" he asked, his tone deceptively light.

"He doesn't just want to arrive at my door with flowers or chocolate and a private note," she insisted.

"I see." He wanted to shake her shoulders and make her confess everything.

She lifted her chin and boldly met his gaze. "We will ride in Hyde Park tomorrow in full view at the promenade hour. Mr. Marbury doesn't care about my past or being seen together. Your attempts have failed."

*I never fail,* he mused.

If she thought she was rid of him, she didn't know his character. She'd given him the perfect opportunity to engage

Marbury *and* watch her.

• • •

Late that night, Gareth met Simon Marbury in Satan's Lair. The gambling club was crowded with well-dressed aristocracy and wealthy middle class financiers, merchants, and industrialists. They rubbed shoulders around gambling tables and wagered vast sums on the roll of the dice or the flip of a card. Strong spirits were served and smoke curled to the ceiling.

Gareth watched as Simon shifted in his seat at the hazard table. The dice rolled on the green baize and Simon lost more than he won.

"I'm done," Gareth said to the croupier.

"I want to keep playing," Simon insisted.

Gareth sipped his brandy. Simon had already lost heavily tonight. First at whist, and now at hazard. He was a heavy gambler, and not a good one from what Gareth had seen. No wonder Simon needed to resort to criminal activities to support his lifestyle.

Gareth suspected Jane had no idea about Simon's gambling. By gambling only at the private male clubs, Simon kept his habit hidden from the ladies of polite society.

"How about a try at *vingt-et-un?*" Gareth suggested.

Simon nodded and set the dice on the table. "I never knew you were a gambler, Ramsey. I've never seen you here before."

Gareth smiled wryly. "I prefer other vices."

"Ah, you like the whores."

Gareth hesitated, weighing Simon. "What man doesn't?

And you?"

"The Seven Sins in Soho is my favorite."

Gareth made himself look blandly at Simon while inside his temper flared. The Seven Sins was known as the worst kind of brothel. It had at least a dozen rooms, each with wall to wall mirrors and every conceivable manual and mechanical device to ensure a customer's sexual gratification. The women were kept like slaves and often beaten. Daniel had previously mentioned a secret investigation against the proprietor to shut down the seedy brothel.

Gareth's gut clenched tight. Jane wanted this man as a lover, probably her first after the suicide of her husband.

Gareth had no standing with Jane, no reason to interfere with her plans to find a lover. Yet he knew one thing to be true: he wouldn't allow it.

A vivid image of their kiss seared his mind. When she'd tripped and fallen into his arms, his heart pounded, his body hardened, and he'd wanted her fiercely.

*Not true,* he thought.

The moment he'd discovered his initials were on her list—despite her protests to the contrary—his pride demanded she rewrite it to place him first.

Or better yet, that his name be the *only* one listed.

The dealer dealt them cards. Simon glanced at his cards and tapped the table. The dealer threw him another card, and Simon's face fell. Gareth was dealt another card and won.

For all Simon's looks, he was skilled at deception—an accomplished actor—behind his foppish façade. But Gareth's work as a barrister had taught him that appearances could be deceiving. Some of the most beautiful ladies, or highly respected gentlemen in the House of Lords, hid the worst secrets.

Simon downed his brandy and motioned for a servant to bring him another. He was intoxicated, betting and losing heavily.

Now was the time. "My client has money to invest," Gareth said.

"How much money?" Simon asked, his words slightly slurred.

"A tidy sum, but it will not be an ordinary investment."

"Meaning?"

"There are rumors you know how to turn a profit."

Simon's glazed eyes narrowed. "And where have you heard such rumors?"

"I'm a barrister, Marbury. I know how to keep a confidence. All my client cares about is your contract with the Ordnance Department to manufacture cannons. That and the fact that some of your cannons are reputed to earn you fast and tidy profits."

A wary expression clouded Simon's face. "I don't know what you're—"

Gareth waved a hand. "I don't care about ethics and neither does my investor. He has twenty thousand pounds."

Simon's red eyes widened. "Twenty thousand pounds?"

"A first installment."

Simon leaned close. "I want to meet this man."

"It's not possible. He does business only through me. Are you interested?"

Simon raised his glass. "I admit I'm intrigued. But I know better than to commit to anything without further discussion."

Marbury was hesitant to trust anyone, even an investor willing to offer a small fortune. Gareth would have to cultivate a friendship with Marbury and slowly earn his trust.

Gareth nodded. "I understand you have concerns."

Simon set his empty glass on the table and stood. "Shall we go to the Seven Sins to talk details?"

# Chapter Five

The following afternoon, Jane met Simon Marbury in Hyde Park. He waved as she approached riding side-saddle on her white mare.

"Good morning Lady Stanwell." Sitting astride his horse, he was dressed in the latest fashionable attire — breeches, top boots, a meticulously tailored olive green coat, and starched cravat. Yet for all his finery, there were faint circles under his eyes, and she wondered how much alcohol he'd consumed after she'd left him the prior evening.

Jane smiled in greeting. "How did you know it was me?"

"Your fetching bonnet does not entirely cover your hair. The fair color is lovely and quite recognizable," he said.

"Thank you, Mr. Marbury."

"You must call me Simon." He motioned to the stretch of gravel roadway. "Shall we?"

The line of carriages on Rotten Row traveled at a slow pace at the fashionable afternoon hour. The sky was a brilliant blue, and sunlight glistened off the Serpentine River. The fragrant scent of flowering shrubs filled the air.

Jane adjusted the skirts of her elegant riding habit as she took in the scene. Her clothing was new, and she'd chosen a forest green that complemented her coloring.

A sporting curricle and several high-perched phaetons dashed by. Passersby stopped to greet friends. The park was the place to be seen, and Jane realized they were attracting a significant amount of attention during the promenade hour. She experienced a moment of unease.

She glanced at Simon. If he was distressed, he did not show it. To the contrary, he sat straight in his saddle, exuding an almost brash confidence, and seemed to enjoy the attention.

"Forgive me for my forwardness, but I find myself drawn to you, Lady Stanwell. You have not attended many society events in a while, have you?"

If he was probing about Charles's suicide, she didn't acknowledge it. Surely Simon Marbury was aware of her reputation as the tragic widow, but for some reason, he had chosen to ignore it and take her for a ride in the park. Now that he'd shown interest, society had opened up to her. It was only the afternoon after Lady Sefton's masquerade, and she'd had two invitations delivered to her home that morning.

How bold could she be?

"You're right. I haven't attended many functions." She tilted her head to the side and regarded him. "May I be truthful?"

"Of course. You must consider me a friend."

She shifted in her saddle. "It's been over two years since my husband's death. I'm tired of the isolation."

"The official mourning period is only one year and one

day," he pointed out.

"True, but I'm aware of the gossip. What people whisper. I want to start over."

"Meaning?"

She met his blue gaze. "I seek excitement."

His nostrils flared slightly. "Tell me what you are looking for."

"I want to live life to its fullest. Experience everything I have been denied. I want fun, pleasure…excitement."

His lips curled in a smile. "I am more than happy to oblige you."

"I understand you are a man who enjoys all the Season has to offer," she said.

"My reputation precedes me, then?"

He asked a question, but his tone suggested he knew exactly what others thought of him and he liked it.

He leaned forward in his saddle, and his blue eyes held hers. "I sense you must be handled delicately."

She wasn't sure what he meant. Was he referring to her isolation from society or her disposition after her husband's suicide?

"We should start slowly. I would be honored if you'd accompany me to the Theatre Royal next week," he said.

Excitement thrummed in her veins. It had been years since she'd attended the theatre. She'd always loved to go, but Charles never had time to escort her. He was always at his clubs, Newmarket, or Tattersalls.

"I'd like that very much," she said.

"Splendid."

Jane glanced at him beneath lowered lashes. His profile was even more striking in the daylight. What would it be like to kiss him?

The thought barely crossed her mind before another followed. How would it compare to the kiss she shared with Gareth Ramsey? Would her pulse leap to life, and a delicious shiver heat her body?

She mentally berated herself. She had to cease thinking of their shared kiss.

*Of him.*

She despised Gareth. He was a brute, a high-handed man who couldn't be controlled.

Completely unlike Simon Marbury.

The sound of galloping hooves drew her attention.

"Hello there!"

Jane whirled around in disbelief to find Gareth approaching astride a big black thoroughbred.

Dear lord! Had she conjured his presence?

Or worse still, had Gareth followed her here? He'd known she would be at the park. She'd told him last night at the ball. A disturbing thought froze in her mind. Had he pulled her onto the terrace and purposely angered her in order to learn when she would next meet Simon? But why would he bother? For some reason she was a challenge to him. There was no other logical explanation.

"Hello, Ramsey. Out for a ride?" Simon asked.

"I find it invigorating. You never know whom you will meet." Gareth nodded at her in greeting, his dark eyes traveling her form. "Good day, Lady Stanwell."

She looked at him in disbelief. He was wearing top-boots and leather breeches which outlined the muscular thighs that gripped the powerful thoroughbred. His navy coat stretched across his broad shoulders, which appeared a mile wide. His big hands held the reins skillfully, his fingers tapered and strong. She remembered what his hands had felt like around her waist, holding her close. What would they feel like if they touched her elsewhere?

"I've never seen you ride in the park at this popular hour," Simon said.

"I'm aware I've avoided the promenade hour. I prefer to ride early in the morning." A faint glint of humor lit Gareth's eyes as he looked at her. "But I realize I've been quite unsocial, and I've decided to turn over a new leaf."

Jane was mortified. She'd said the same words to him in Lady Sefton's library.

He was trying to intimidate her. His unspoken words were loud and clear: *I know your secrets.*

She stiffened her spine and gripped her reins tightly. If he thought to scare her with his knowledge of her list, then he would soon learn of her mettle.

"What an interesting choice of words, Mr. Ramsey," she said, her tone light.

Gareth cocked a dark eyebrow mockingly. "You don't believe in starting over, Lady Stanwell?"

She met his gaze without flinching. "To the contrary, I very much believe in it. I just didn't think a man of your advanced years would trouble yourself."

Simon burst out laughing. "The lady has wit, Ramsey. Pray tell me, what did you do to earn her ire?"

Gareth shrugged. "Nothing I can think of. My friend Lord Kirkland married her cousin, Lady Sophia, last year. Some would consider us almost family."

Jane gaped. Family was the last word she would choose to describe Gareth Ramsey.

But Simon clearly found the entire exchange humorous. "Come," he said, urging his mount down the path. "It's too nice an afternoon to spend it bickering."

They rode together for the next few minutes, chatting about nonsensical matters. It was clear Gareth wouldn't move onward.

Jane found it difficult to meet Gareth's gaze. Her eyes kept dropping to his mouth—his full sensual lips—and the memory of his infuriating kiss returned. Her skin prickled in awareness, and her pulse beat in her throat.

It was bad enough he knew about her list, but must she constantly relive the rest of what had occurred in the library?

They were more than halfway through the park when a group of gentlemen waved in the distance. "Marbury!"

"Pardon me for a moment. I have a wager to discuss with Lord Wheeler and Lord Closter." Simon said.

As soon as Simon rode off to greet his friends, Jane whirled to face Gareth. "Why are you here? And don't tell me you wanted fresh air."

"I cannot stop thinking about your list," Gareth said.

Her mind spun. "A gentleman would keep a lady's secret."

"Your secret is safe with me. But I find that I cannot stay away from you."

An undeniable magnetism was building between them. "Why?"

Reaching out, he snatched her reins from her hands and led her horse down a meandering pathway into a secluded grove of shady trees.

Panic rose up her throat. "What are you *doing*?" she cried out.

He peered at her intently. "Don't you feel it?"

"Feel what?"

"The attraction. Don't tell me you didn't enjoy our kiss last night."

A tingling began in the pit of her stomach. She shook her head in denial. "I did not."

"Liar."

"You're crazed."

"Come now, Jane. You were a married woman. Surely you can recognize desire…passion."

Her face grew warm and heaven help her—she felt a lurch of excitement. "Do not speak to me like that. It's entirely improper."

He studied her closely, too closely. "Unless you haven't experienced passion. Was your husband unskilled?"

He was too intuitive. She didn't want to share anything about her marriage, and certainly not with him. "Stop this at once."

"He wasn't skilled, then. Was he incompetent in bed?" Gareth said.

"Stop it!"

"I can't. You're even more intriguing than I thought. Let me show you what it can be like between a man and a woman. Between us." Still holding her mare's reins, he urged the thoroughbred close until his muscular thigh grazed her skirts.

He looked at her as if he wanted to strip her naked, toss her to the ground, and have his way with her in the secluded grove. The thought should repulse her. Instead his nearness made her senses spin and her heart pound. Whatever feelings she had for him, they seemed to be growing, and she was more shaken than she cared to admit.

"No," she said firmly. "I don't want you. I want Mr. Marbury."

A muscle ticked angrily at his jaw at the mention of Simon's name. Gareth had exhibited the same physical reaction last night when she'd purposely flirted with Simon at the refreshment table.

"Why Marbury?" he ground out.

Why indeed? With Gareth Ramsey staring down at her with those dark eyes she couldn't think.

Couldn't breathe.

Her body felt heavy and warm. She desperately needed to put distance between them. "There are too many people in the park. Anyone can see us," she protested.

He shook his head. "We're well hidden. And I find it hard to believe you care. You caused quite a scene waltzing with Marbury last night and riding with him today."

"Who I dance with or who I choose to meet in the park is none of your concern."

His eyes narrowed, and a shiver raced down her spine.

"You plan to see him again, don't you?" he demanded.

"Yes, he's taking me to the theatre next week," she blurted out angrily, then bit her lip as soon as she realized what she'd revealed. He knew too much, was too shrewd, too cunning. She opened her mouth to argue, but Gareth tugged on her horse's reins.

Caught unaware, Jane lurched forward as her mare started. She grasped the pommel to prevent herself from falling as Gareth led them back on the main path.

She flashed him a look of disdain. "Don't you ever do that—"

Gareth dropped her horse's reins. "Careful, my lady. Marbury returns."

She turned to see that Simon had indeed left his friends and was riding back to them. She was furious with Gareth, and even angrier with herself for her loose tongue and her physical reaction toward the infuriating man.

She was careful to avoid eye contact with Gareth for the remainder of the ride. At last they reached the end of the roadway.

Gareth turned to Simon. "Don't forget we have business to discuss."

Simon nodded. "I'm interested, Ramsey, but I still have questions."

"I'll be in touch to talk privately," Gareth said.

Jane looked back and forth between the two men. What business could they possibly have together?

She didn't want to know. Her concern was Simon. She wanted nothing to do with Gareth.

They left the park and came to the street where traffic was heavy. Elegant curricles and carriages moved alongside rattling hackneys and heavy brewers' carts driven by men in leather aprons.

Just then a small scrap of a boy darted past and startled the horses. Simon's horse reared upward, his hooves inches from the boy's head.

Gareth jumped off his thoroughbred and yanked the boy from danger just as the horse's hooves came crashing down, narrowly missing Gareth's shoulder.

"My God! Are you all right?" Simon asked.

Gareth nodded tersely then turned to the boy. "Have a care where you're going, son."

"Sorry, guv'nor. The cart dropped an apple." The boy's brown eyes were wide in his dirt-smudged face. His shirt was stained and his trousers ripped at one knee. He looked like he could use a bath and a good meal.

Gareth pulled his purse from inside his coat and gave the boy a gold coin. "Buy yourself a hot meal."

The boy's eyes grew enormous. His small fist clenched around the coin and he sprinted across the street and disappeared in the throng of traffic.

"Ungrateful wretch," Simon said. "They don't belong near the park."

"He was scared and hungry," Gareth said. "It wasn't the boy's fault."

Jane knew there were poor, starving children in the city, but she'd never literally stumbled across one. She wanted to chase after the boy, see that he was bathed, fed, and had a warm bed for the night.

She turned to Gareth instead. He'd acted swiftly, risking injury to save the child. "Thank you, Mr. Ramsey."

"You were never in harm's way, my lady," Gareth pointed out.

Jane looked at him incredulously. "Not for me—for saving the boy's life."

Gareth approached her seated on her horse. "It was in my power to help him. Wouldn't you have done the same?"

Jane swallowed. "I would hope so. But you put yourself directly in harm's way to save another. I don't know if I'd have the courage."

"I don't doubt you would."

His words made her heart pound. She regarded him with heightened curiosity, and she longed to reach out and trace her finger down his chiseled jaw. She couldn't stop herself from wondering about his true character. How could a man be so infuriating one minute, then act so valiantly the next?

. . .

Gareth watched as Jane and Simon disappeared down the street. Simon intended to escort her home, and Gareth had experienced a stab of jealousy as Simon led her away.

Jane was proving to be a challenge with her wit and beauty. She wanted a lover and an adventure. He strongly suspected her husband had been either unskilled or uninterested in his young wife's pleasure in the bedroom.

She was a fascinating contradiction. She acted the worldly widow seeking a liaison, but she was naive when it came to the dissolute interests of the men of the *ton*. All the men on her list, especially Simon Marbury, were depraved and completely unsuitable in Gareth's opinion.

He had to take care that he not lose sight of his mission. He had already taken steps to befriend Simon Marbury. Their night at the gambling hell and brothel still hadn't resulted in a firm agreement from Simon to enter into business. Gareth needed to gain Simon's trust, to entice him to do business with his "mystery investor." He'd have to get closer to Simon, play upon his greed and spendthrift ways. The man was a reckless gambler who spent lavish amounts of money on his clothing. Simon needed money, and his avaricious nature would be his downfall.

If Simon was interested in Jane, then Gareth would use that interest to get closer to Simon. He'd already been successful in prying Jane for information. He'd appeared at the park today, and he'd learned about her future trip to the theatre with Marbury. But Gareth would have to be careful.

Jane was no fool. If he kept showing up whenever she was out with Marbury, she would suspect there was more to Gareth's appearances that just a man pursuing a woman he desired.

He wanted to seduce Jane and keep her away from Marbury. But his mission required that he cultivate a friendship with Simon and gain his trust. Only then could he learn how many others were involved in the conspiracy to supply inferior cannons to English troops.

He would do what was necessary, and he never had qualms about whom he'd used in the past to accomplish his missions. During his last assignment, he'd developed a friendship with a judge in order to prove the man guilty of accepting bribes from defense barristers. Gareth's conscience hadn't suffered, even when the man was arrested before his family and carted off to Newgate.

His friends, Daniel and Robert, thought him cold, calculating, and emotionless. The truth was Gareth didn't give a rat's arse about other peoples opinions. He understood his mission, his duty.

He worked for the Crown, for the common Englishman. Simon was the worst sort of criminal—a man who didn't care if he gravely wounded or even killed his own countrymen, young soldiers who risked their lives to protect citizens.

Gareth may desire Jane, but it didn't change who he was or what he needed to accomplish. His personal feelings had never affected his performance, and he wouldn't allow his lust to overcome his good sense, no matter how tempting the lady.

# Chapter Six

Jane woke in the middle of the night reliving the sound of the gunshot.

She bolted upright in bed, her legs tangled in the bed sheets, her coverlet strewn across the floor. Beads of perspiration formed on her brow, and her nightgown clung to her damp skin. Leaning over the side of the bed, she took in great gulps of air.

The nightmare always ended the same. She would find Charles on the floor of his study, a flurry of blood-splattered vouchers for his precious horses spread across the Oriental carpet. He had pressed the pistol against his temple and pulled the trigger. Bits of skull, hair, and brain added to the gore.

Charles, with his reddish-brown hair, brown eyes, and jovial laugh, had looked nothing like his former self in death.

The mantle clock had chimed. It ticked in her mind—four full strokes before she'd taken in the horrid scene, and her screams had echoed throughout the house to send the servants running.

Dear lord, would the nightmares ever cease?

Jane closed her eyes, breathed in through her nose then out through her mouth.

A knock on her bedchamber door reverberated through the room and made her start.

"Jane? Are you all right?" Eleanor opened the door. Dressed in a cotton nightrail, barefoot, and without her customary lace cap, she approached the bed. Resting her cane on the bed frame, her wrinkled brow was deeply furrowed. "I heard you scream," she said, her voice laced with concern.

Had she screamed out loud?

"I'm sorry," Jane whispered.

Her aunt sat on the edge of the bed and smoothed Jane's hair. "Never apologize, darling. Was it the same dream?"

Unable to answer, Jane swallowed the lump in her throat and nodded.

"Oh, Jane. This will pass, I promise."

Jane stifled a sob. "I can't help but wonder if I could have prevented him from—"

"No. What happened to Charles was not your fault. You were a devoted wife."

Jane had been infatuated with her young, handsome husband, but it hadn't been enough to lure him away from Tattersall's or every other horse track.

The truth behind his suicide had cut like a surgeon's blade. She had known all along, hadn't she? Charles had loved his horses far more than he had ever loved her.

If only she had conceived a child, it would have made Charles's death more bearable. A baby to lavish with love. A child of her own. But that would never happen.

"It's time to move on, Jane. You've started to do so already. Do not let what happened hold you back any longer," Eleanor said.

Jane took a deep breath. She was weak by nature. She fell in love too easily, trusted too quickly.

*But no more.*

Her aunt was right. Her doomed marriage was in the past. She would not repeat her mistakes.

After Eleanor left, Jane sat at the window seat overlooking the street. It was near dawn, and the first rays of light touched the sky. In the distance the tolling of a church bell sounded, uplifting and inspiring.

For the first time, she had a purpose.

She had already begun to put the past behind her. She would find a lover, a man who could show her pleasure rather than demand his own, and most importantly, a man who would not break her heart the way Charles had.

• • •

The following morning, Jane sat in the library reading when Graves, her butler, entered.

"Lady Olivia is here to see you."

Jane rose. "Please see her in and send tea, Graves."

She was returning the book to the library shelves when Olivia entered the room. Dressed in a pink walking dress with puff sleeves and an embroidered lace hem, her friend looked as fresh as a garden rose.

"I cannot wait another moment. How was your ride in the park with Mr. Marbury?" Olivia said.

Jane smiled weakly. "It went well."

As long as she didn't think of Gareth Ramsey.

Olivia sat on a gold sofa and patted the seat for Jane to join her. "You don't expect me to be satisfied with that answer, do you?"

Jane joined her friend on the sofa. "Simon invited me to the theatre."

"How exciting! Has he kissed you yet?"

"Olivia!"

Olivia giggled. "I can't help it. This is all so exciting and well past due for you."

Jane hesitated. "Simon hasn't kissed me, but I've kissed another." An unbidden memory of rugged features and bone melting kisses made her blood soar. Gareth's lips been hot and seductive and she'd never felt such raw passion. She could still recall the warmth and hardness of his chest.

Olivia gaped. "Who?"

"Gareth Ramsey." As soon as Jane said the name, she felt a sense of relief that she could finally confide the secret to her friend.

Olivia's brow knit. "Baron Suffolk's youngest son? The barrister who obtained a divorce for Viscount Harrison?"

"Yes." Jane wasn't surprised Olivia knew the details.

The door opened and Graves wheeled in a tea tray. Olivia waited until the butler departed and they were alone again. "I wasn't even aware you liked Mr. Ramsey," Olivia said.

"I don't." *Not really.*

Jane poured two cups of tea and handed one to Olivia.

Her friend took a quick sip, then set her cup down on her saucer and leaned forward in her seat. "How was Mr.

Ramsey's kiss?" Olivia asked, an eager expression lighting her face.

*Searing. Passionate. Knee-buckling.* "Pleasant."

Olivia eyed her. "Pleasant? That's it?"

"All right. Much more than pleasant," Jane admitted.

"That's wonderful!"

"No, it's not. I have a problem. Gareth found my list at Lady Sefton's masquerade. I've never been more humiliated."

Olivia gasped. "Has he told anyone?"

Jane bit her lower lip. "He says he won't."

But the nagging in the back of her mind refused to be stilled. The truth was she didn't know Gareth's intentions, and she certainly didn't trust him.

Olivia nodded as if she had complete faith in Jane's answer. "A true gentleman would never reveal a lady's secret."

Despite being the son of a baron, Gareth didn't behave like a gentleman. He'd pulled her into a private alcove at the park. And he'd kissed her against her will at the masquerade.

*Not entirely true.* He may have made the first move, but a part of her had longed for him to continue to kiss her.

He was a mystery. Perhaps that was the attraction. She'd thought him arrogant and high handed one moment, only to witness an incident like the one today with the boy in the street. Gareth's actions were heroic, and he'd risked serious injury to save an impoverished child. She grudgingly admitted he possessed admirable qualities.

But that didn't mean she wanted him as her lover.

"You'll soon have your pick of men," Olivia said.

"I don't need to pick. I've already chosen Simon Marbury."

Olivia gave her a familiar look—one she'd often given

her during their childhood when she'd been exasperated with Jane. "There's no need to rush into a decision. I realize Mr. Ramsey wasn't initially on your list."

He *had* been on her list. But that wasn't something she wanted to confess to her friend.

"I fear Gareth won't leave me be. He says he wants to... to fill the position."

Olivia clasped her hands together. "Wonderful! You should be wooed and pursued."

"Yes, but not by him. Simon has asked me to attend the theatre, and I intend to take full advantage." She would purge Gareth Ramsey from her mind. She was convinced that once she was with Simon, it shouldn't be difficult.

# Chapter Seven

Jane rested her gloved hand on Simon Marbury's arm as he escorted her into the crowded lobby of the Theatre Royale on Drury Lane. The theatre was stunning with black and white marble floors and high, arched ceilings. Large chandeliers and wall sconces illuminated velvet draperies and gilt moldings. The scent of French perfumes and spicy colognes filled the warm entry.

Jane followed Simon's lead and surveyed her surroundings. Women dressed in colorful silks, polished pumps, and sparkling jewels chatted behind fluttering fans. Some of the gentlemen wore simple black and white evening attire while others strutted about like peacocks in spotted and flowered waistcoats, ridiculously high-pointed shirtfronts, or a diamond stickpin holding an intricately knotted cravat in place.

Simon's clothing rivaled the most impressive of dandies. Dressed in a coat of claret kerseymere and checked waistcoat with brass buttons, his pocket watch hung heavy with numerous ornamental fobs and gold seals. Jane didn't miss the sidelong gazes of the women when Simon approached. Several men waved openly in greeting.

Jane realized they were causing a bit of a stir. Surely gossip would ensue. But after their ride in Hyde Park, many already knew she was "officially" out of mourning and had captured the attention of Simon Marbury.

Simon placed his hand over hers. "I do enjoy the theatre."

She suspected he relished being watched by the theatre patrons more than he enjoyed the play. Just like their ride in the park, Simon thrived on the attention. She could just imagine the gossip: the startlingly handsome Simon Marbury taking pity on Lady Stanwell, the tragic widow.

It certainly made for good theatre.

"Shall we take our seats?" he said.

Simon led her to his private box and sat beside her.

Anticipation thrummed through Jane's veins. It had been so long since she'd attended a play. She leaned forward and clutched the balustrade, watching the people as they all began to take their seats, and the adjoining boxes as they filled with well-dressed theatergoers and their families. Below she spotted a group of dandies seated close to the orchestra. They were a boisterous lot, chatting and waving at each other. Across the way she spotted older matrons who frowned in disapproval at the rambunctious men. In the front row, a young couple with the flush of new love on their faces held hands and whispered to each other behind their programs.

*Oh, to be so young and ignorant*. She prayed their infatuation would last. Especially the man's.

She spotted another couple. The man gaped at a woman

wearing a low-bodice who took the seat in front of him. His wife glared at him and slapped his arm with her fan.

Jane's giggle died on her lips when an unmistakable tall, dark-haired man entered the theatre. Her heat skipped a beat.

Gareth Ramsey.

Had he followed her? If so, then she was entirely at fault. She'd blurted out that Simon was escorting her to the theatre when Gareth had confronted her at Hyde Park.

Jane stared, her emotions a whirlwind inside her. She couldn't possibly be excited at his presence.

Could she?

Then Gareth turned and smiled at an attractive chestnut-haired lady. He waited for the woman to take her seat before sitting beside her.

Jane's stomach clenched as comprehension dawned. Gareth was with another woman.

Her fingers tightened on the railing. Vivid images of their encounter in the park rushed back to her. Gareth had been so bold, pulling her horse aside into an isolated spot. He had made her furious, and yet…a deep part of her was thrilled that a man had shown that much interest in her.

And Gareth wasn't just any man. Something about his sharp, confident profile and muscular body captured her attention. She should be wary of his size, let alone his domineering nature, but when his coffee-brown eyes gazed at her in the alcove, her skin had grown hot and her pulse had leapt.

Then there was the incident with the boy as they'd left the park. Gareth had acted swiftly as if he'd been trained to deal with just such an urgent incident. There was more to him than a barrister and estranged son of a baron. He'd risked his safety so easily, whereas Simon had been unable to control his horse and had blamed the child. Jane continued to stare below—she couldn't help herself—until minutes later Gareth looked up and their gazes caught.

The corner of his mouth curled in a lazy smile.

She sucked in a breath and turned away.

"I like Hamlet best," Simon said.

"Pardon?" She'd momentarily forgotten where she was and who accompanied her.

"I said tonight's performance of Hamlet is one of my favorites."

Jane nodded, not trusting her voice. She worried Simon would notice her distress—and interest in the theatre's other patrons.

Thankfully, the lights dimmed and the curtain lifted to reveal a backdrop of a medieval Danish castle. Moments later, the actors—two castle sentries—came on stage. Jane struggled to keep her attention on the performance. She sneaked glances beneath lowered lashes at Gareth and the lady who sat beside him.

The pair leaned toward each other and exchanged words. Jane's stomach tightened a fraction more.

Simon touched her arm, just above where her glove ended and below her sleeve. Her skin prickled in awareness.

She turned to find Simon's sapphire eyes watching her. "I'm glad you were able to accompany me tonight, my lady." He leaned close and touched her exposed skin. "I do believe we will have a close relationship. I'm prepared to offer you even more excitement than you ever thought possible."

...

Gareth knew the precise moment Jane spotted him. She looked exquisite dressed in a yellow gown with her golden hair in an elegant top knot that accentuated the cat-like tilt to her brown eyes. Her attention was presently on the stage, but Gareth suspected she was paying little attention to the play.

*Look at me.*

Instead she turned to Simon and smiled at something he said. Gareth felt like he'd been punched in the gut, his jealousy was so overwhelming. He wanted to be the one sitting beside her in the private box whispering sweet words in her ear.

Not sweet, but erotic.

He had known she would be in attendance tonight, but he hated seeing her alone with Marbury in the private box.

"The lady noticed you, then?"

Gareth turned to his guest for the evening. Lady Weatherby was a middle-aged widow of a baron who often aided the Home Office with special requests. She was attractive, with an abundance of brown curls, green eyes, and a voluptuous figure. She was present tonight to help him with his mission.

Gareth scowled. "Is it that obvious?" He'd always prided himself on hiding his emotions. But there was something tantalizing about Jane that drew him, though he knew she was a distraction he could not afford. This maddening attraction put his cold efficiency and tightly leashed control in jeopardy.

Lady Weatherby shrugged a shoulder. "Don't worry, no on else has noticed. I'm trained to observe these things."

"Duly noted," Gareth said dryly.

Hamlet's voice rose dramatically on stage as he complained his mother fell into "incestuous sheets" with her brother-in-law too swiftly after the death of Hamlet's father.

Lady Weatherby touched his sleeve and drew Gareth's attention back to her. Leaning close, she whispered in his ear. "I must say that you're as tightly wound as a clock spring, Gareth. You needn't deny yourself pleasure this evening."

Gareth forced his shoulders to ease. Lady Weatherby had made her intentions clear, but he wasn't interested in slating his lust this evening.

At least not with her.

"Another time, Kate," he said.

A consummate professional, she smiled and leaned back in her seat. "When do you want me to engage Mr. Marbury?"

"I'll let you know."

It turned out they didn't have to wait long. Partway through the play, as Hamlet's behavior became more and more erratic, Simon rose from his seat.

"Now," Gareth said.

• • •

Gareth descended the theatre stairs to the vestibule. Only a few people were present, those seeking the retiring rooms or others wanting a break from the play to smoke cheroots.

He scanned the area and spotted Marbury speaking with a man. They stood in the far corner, away from the bright light of the chandeliers, and shadows hid the man's face. Gareth couldn't make out his identity, and he wondered if he had anything to do with Marbury's criminal activities.

The unknown man was dressed in a dark colors, and before Gareth reached the last step, the man turned and walked out the theatre doors.

Gareth wanted to pursue him, but it was impossible to pass by Simon without being observed. Frustration roiled inside Gareth for letting a possible lead walk away, but he quickly refocused. His true purpose was to meet with Simon privately.

Gareth strode directly to him. "Good to see you again, Marbury."

A flicker of surprise crossed Simon's face. "Hello again, Ramsey. I didn't expect to see you here."

"I admit the theatre is not my favorite past time, but I'm here tonight out of obligation. Duty requires I escort a relative."

Marbury chuckled. "I understand. Familial duty and responsibility can be quite tedious at times. My mother has been more demanding since my father took ill." Simon waved a glass of champagne he'd been holding. "But it's good I ran into you."

"Oh?'

"I've carefully considered your client's offer. I believe I'm favorable to it," Simon said.

Gareth felt an immediate sense of satisfaction. This was what he'd been waiting for. "I'm happy to hear it. I've been in contact with my client, and he has some questions for you."

"When can I come to your Gray's Inn chambers?" Simon asked.

"Tomorrow afternoon. I'll tell my clerk to expect you."

Simon nodded. "Until then."

Out of the corner of his eye, Gareth saw the door to

the ladies' retiring room open and Lady Weatherby step outside. She gave him a discrete nod and stayed by the door. She knew not to approach until Gareth departed. He had confidence the voluptuous widow could easily delay Marbury long enough for Gareth to see to his second task of the evening.

Gareth glanced at the glass of champagne Simon was holding. "There are servants to fetch whatever you want," he said.

Simon shrugged and smiled. "I needed to stretch my legs."

*And to talk to someone,* Gareth thought.

Even though he wasn't able to pursue the man Simon had been speaking with, Gareth still counted the evening a success. Simon trusted him enough to come to his chambers tomorrow and enter into a business arrangement.

Gareth's thoughts turned to Jane alone in the private theatre box. Excitement thrummed in his veins.

Now he'd attend to his second task for the evening.

• • •

Jane shifted in her seat as she sat alone in the box. After Simon had excused himself to fetch her a glass of champagne, her thoughts immediately returned to the guests below. She leaned forward, scanning the seats for signs of Gareth and his lady friend.

Both chairs were empty.

Her thoughts turned cold. Had Gareth and the woman left the performance without her noticing? Were they lovers who had departed to be together?

And why did she care? To make things worse, added

to her disappointment were feelings of guilt. She was here tonight as Simon's guest. She shouldn't be thinking of Gareth.

Footsteps sounded behind her. Jane quickly pasted a smile on her face and turned to greet Simon.

Gareth Ramsey entered the box instead.

Shock flew through her, and she jumped to her feet. "What the devil!"

"Shh." He grasped her arm and pulled her deep into the box, behind the curtains, away from any prying eyes. He wore a dark blue coat that heightened his ruggedly handsome features. Her heart hammered foolishly as a shudder heated her body at his nearness.

She tugged on her arm. "You're insane! This is entirely improper," she hissed.

"No one can see or hear us."

"My escort will return," she protested.

"Not for a while."

"How on earth could you know that?"

"I know," he said, a cold edge of irony in his voice.

Gareth Ramsey was brash and infuriating. He was also a tall dark-haired devil who brought her senses to life. "You can't keep pulling me into secluded corners at your whim."

"You never answered my question in the park."

Her mind faltered. "What question?"

"Why choose Simon Marbury to be your lover?"

She was caught off guard by the sudden intensity of his gaze. He'd barged into a private box and hauled her behind a curtain just to ask her *that?*

"It's none of your concern. Besides, why should you care? You're escorting a lady tonight." Her voice sounded shrewish to her own ears.

He arched a dark eyebrow. "Jealous, are you?"

"Never. Just pointing out a fact."

"She's my cousin."

She looked at him in disbelief. "Your cousin? Don't you dare treat me like a fool—"

"You *are* jealous."

Narrowing her eyes, she pointed to the exit. "Get out."

"Not without a price."

"A price?"

"A kiss."

She gasped. "You arrogant oaf!"

He pulled her into his arms.

As soon as he touched her, her skin sizzled and she felt an immediate and total attraction. Panic followed, welling in her throat. "We will be discovered."

"No, we won't."

She looked up into his eyes. "Why do you insist upon a kiss?"

Reaching out, he trailed a finger down her cheek. "You intrigue me. I want to be your lover. Burn your list, Jane. Let me be the one."

Her heart raced. She watched in fascinated horror as he lowered his head. His lips were soft and warm as they brushed hers. She should push him away. Instead, a blast of heat skittered along her nerves and her lips parted. He took advantage and thrust his tongue inside to explore her mouth. Her hands settled on his shoulders and his muscles flexed beneath her fingers. He groaned and pressed her closer. She gasped as her soft curves molded fully against the hard planes of his body. It felt forbidden and delicious and she wanted more. She forgot they were only hidden behind a curtain and that Simon could return at any moment. She forgot everything but the pleasure of his kiss.

His large hands ran down her sides, skimming her breasts. The pleasure was as intense as it was shocking. Then his hand cupped her breast and his thumb grazed her sensitive nipple. Shivers of delight traveled down her spine.

He would be skilled, no doubt. But she couldn't trust him. She would never trust any man again. Every instinct in her body told her that Gareth Ramsey was dangerous. Not in a physical sense. She didn't fear his strength and size, but there were other kinds of wounds, emotional ones, and she'd sworn never to allow herself to lose control of her emotions again.

No. An affair with Gareth Ramsey would be perilous.

Breaking the kiss, she pushed against his hard chest. "No," she said as firmly as she could.

He pulled back, his eyes dark with desire. "Then I insist on pursuing you and changing your mind."

Her composure was a fragile shell around her. He made her feel weak and warm and she had to put an end to these feelings once and for all.

Her chin jutted forward, and she met his eyes. "Suit your-self, Mr. Ramsey. But your efforts will lead you nowhere."

"A challenge, Jane? I accept."

He bowed mockingly, then turned and faded into the darkness.

• • •

Jane heard footsteps, but this time it was Simon who entered the box.

He carried two glasses of champagne and offered her one. "I apologize for the delay. I met an acquaintance in the lobby." Simon's voice was odd, but her disposition was too shaky to care.

Jane raised the glass and took a long sip to calm her nerves. Goodness! Her breathing was still ragged, her thoughts a tumble of confused emotions. Her body still thrummed with the pleasure of Gareth's kiss. Gareth's touch.

The remainder of the performance was long and torturous for Jane. The most dramatic parts of the play—when Hamlet killed his uncle and then died himself—held little interest for her. She kept sneaking looks at Gareth below with the woman whom he claimed to be his cousin. Jane watched the pair to see if they were romantically involved, but saw nothing to indicate they were lovers.

Was Gareth lying to her? Did he truly find her intriguing? Did he really want to be her lover? Or had she just become a conquest because she'd refused him?

It didn't matter either way. Nothing must happen between them. She feared the way her pulse leapt with excitement whenever he was near. Feared what those emotions could make her do. She never wanted to fall under a man's spell again.

At last the lengthy Shakespearean tragedy was over. Simon escorted her outside the theatre to his waiting carriage. Thankfully, there was no sign of Gareth Ramsey or the chestnut haired woman. A footman lowered the step and she climbed inside. Simon settled beside her on the padded bench.

"Thank you for a lovely evening," she said.

"It was just the beginning. I have more outings planned."

"Why agree to take me?"

"It's no secret I find you attractive…and quite interesting."

He spoke of her as if she were an oddity, a rare challenge to a man of his standing.

His gaze lowered to her mouth. "I'd like to kiss you."

She couldn't help but find it ironic that for more than two years, no man had looked upon her with interest or had wanted to kiss her.

Now two men sought to kiss her in one night.

As Simon gazed down at her expectantly, Jane forced herself to relax. This was what she wanted, she told herself. A kiss. And it would be wonderfully passionate.

So much so that she'd forget all about Gareth Ramsey and the insane attraction she felt for the dominant, over-bearing man.

Simon lowered his mouth to hers. The pressure of his lips was pleasant, similar to the first time Charles had kissed her. The scent of his cologne was a bit cloying, unlike the clean shaving soap and fresh outdoors scent of another. She pushed the intrusive thoughts aside. Leaning into Simon, she wrapped her arms around his shoulders.

At her touch, Simon moaned, pulled her closer, and the kiss changed. His tongue penetrated her mouth, his teeth mashed against hers, and for a startling moment she feared she wouldn't be able to breathe. Blessedly, he lifted his head, but her relief was short lived as he licked the column of her throat, leaving a slick path on her skin.

To her dismay, Simon's kisses were nothing like the pleasure she'd experienced in Gareth Ramsey's arms. And Simon's wiry build felt nothing like Gareth's broad, muscular chest. There had been no mistaking the rush of desire she'd felt in Gareth's embrace. It reminded her of the passion she'd heard about in the ladies' retiring room and from her gossiping servants.

She placed her hand against Simon's chest. His heart was pounding, his breathing ragged.

The carriage stopped in front of her town house. Simon's face was in half shadow from the carriage lamp.

"I have not made a mistake about you, my lady. You are almost ready."

Her brow creased. Ready for what? Was he referring to an illicit liaison?

"It's quite late. I fear I'm tired tonight," she found herself saying.

A dark flicker crossed his face as he bent to kiss her gloved hand, and she feared she had insulted him, but when he raised his head, the smooth smile was back in place. "I understand."

She was grateful he didn't press for more intimacy tonight. She needed to go inside and calm her racing thoughts. And her confusion.

"I want you to meet my friends. We are going to Vauxhall Gardens later this week. Will you accompany me?" he said.

She was surprised by the request. It seemed he wasn't put off by her refusal to invite him inside her home.

Simon stared at her, waiting for her answer.

"Of course. I'd be delighted to accompany you." If her smile was slightly strained, he didn't notice.

# Chapter Eight

Gareth met Daniel Forster early the next morning at the foot of the stairs outside St. Bartholomew's hospital.

"I received your note," Gareth said.

Together they started up the stone steps leading into the building. "There's a patient who can provide useful information for the mission," Daniel said.

As soon as they entered, the odors of sweat and vomit mingled with the strong scent of turpentine assailed them. One of Gareth's earlier missions had required him to visit injured soldiers fortunate enough to make it back to London after surviving Waterloo. He'd enjoyed talking with the soldiers, but at the same time he'd come to dread the hospital.

They made him feel as if he were suffocating, the walls containing every sort of human suffering. The scene never changed, only the faces of the doctors and the nurses. The grieving families often huddled in corners, trying desperately not to give up hope.

They walked down a long hallway and passed a doctor with thick spectacles who was clutching a black bag. Nurses rushed to and from rooms.

"How are you progressing with Marbury?" Daniel asked.

"I've told him I have a client who wishes to invest in his company, but remain anonymous. Someone who's interested in turning a quick profit, no questions asked. Marbury insisted on going to the Seven Sins to discuss details. He was more amicable afterwards, but he still has not committed."

Daniel eyed him. "That seedy brothel?"

"It's Marbury's favorite. I stayed downstairs and gambled." Gareth had never visited the brothel in the past and hadn't given it much thought. Even if Daniel succeeded in arresting the proprietor and shutting down the place, another establishment would open soon after. What bothered him the most was that Jane intended to make Simon her lover. She had no idea Simon frequented such a sordid place.

"Do you think Marbury will take the bait?" Daniel said.

"I do. I'm meeting him tomorrow in my chambers to finalize a deal."

"Good." They turned a corner and stopped in front of a door. "This is it," Daniel said.

They entered a long room with half a dozen beds. The patient in the first bed caught Gareth's attention. The man was young, no more than twenty years, with a head of straw-colored hair. Gareth's gaze immediately went to a bandaged stump, what had once been the man's right leg.

"Good morning, Private Stevens," Daniel said.

The soldier turned to the doorway where Gareth and Daniel stood. Cuts and bruises marred his face. One eye was swollen shut.

Daniel motioned to Gareth. "This is Mr. Ramsey. We have a few more questions for you."

Stevens nodded at Daniel. "I'll do the best I can, Lord Clayborne."

Gareth's jaw set as he approached the bedside. The man was too young to suffer the loss of his leg. Gareth had known men who had died from the same injury. Stevens was lucky to be close to London at the time of the accident. If he had been on the battlefield, he would surely have perished from loss of blood.

"You've told me your story, but please tell it again for Mr. Ramsey," Daniel said.

The soldier's good eye turned to Gareth. "We were training, sir. My company received four new cannons. My superior ordered us to fire them during our routine drills. I loaded the cannon and the explosives just like we were trained. I lit the fuse and there was a loud explosion. I remember being hurled through the air and the shock of it... the shock of something tearing into my leg. I hit the ground and then it all went black. I don't remember anything else. Until I woke from the pain. The unbearable pain." He choked as his eyes traveled to the stump.

"You mentioned four new cannons. Did the others malfunction on their users?" Gareth asked.

"No. Ours was the last to be fired. The others functioned properly," Stevens said.

"Do you remember the make of the cannon you used?" Daniel asked.

"They were all Marbury cannons, my lord."

"Thank you, private. I know this is difficult for you,"

Daniel said.

Stevens stared at them with his good eye. "We were training. I never even made it to battle."

"I promise you that we're going to investigate the faulty cannon," Daniel said.

"But how will I work, my lord? I married Bessie just before the accident. She's expecting our first babe," the soldier's voice cracked.

Gareth's gut clenched. Simon Marbury would pay for ruining this young man's life.

Gareth reached out to clasp the private's shoulder. "Don't worry. I need a secretary at my Gray's Inn chambers and I promise that you will always find work. Think only of your recovery for now."

Daniel and Gareth left the hospital.

"Not all Marbury cannons are defective," Daniel said. "One out of four was inferior to that specific regiment. Simon Marbury is bribing the military inspectors and possibly their superiors, and we can't arrest him until we identify everyone involved. If Marbury is questioned before then, he'll undoubtedly argue that since all his cannons passed inspection, the failure must not be from a manufacturing defect."

Gareth nodded. "I have an appointment to meet with Simon tomorrow. Marbury has weaknesses, and I plan to exploit them to learn the truth."

. . .

At precisely two o'clock the following afternoon, Simon Marbury entered Gareth's Gray's Inn chambers.

"Please sit," Gareth said, motioning to a chair before his

mahogany desk. He rose and went to a sideboard in the corner of his office, poured two glasses of whiskey, and handed one to Simon.

Sipping the alcohol, Simon surveyed Gareth's chambers and noted the large desk, the stack of litigation documents with polished stone paperweights on a side Pembroke table, and the brass scales of justice on the mantle.

"I never thought I'd be in need of a barrister. My solicitor handles all my legal business," Simon said.

"Thankfully you do not need my legal services. Consider me a liaison between my client and you," Gareth said.

Simon turned away from the mantle. "I admit this is a first for me. I have always met my business investors face-to-face."

"As I said before, my client prefers to remain anonymous. He feels his initial investment of twenty thousand pounds is sufficient for you to trust him."

The Home Office had provided the money. Daniel understood it would take a considerable amount of blunt to entice Marbury to conduct business with an unknown partner. Simon needed the money. It was Gareth's job to coax him into accepting it.

"My investor is smart and influential. He approached me and said there was no shrewder business owner than Simon Marbury."

Simon eyes shone bright. "He isn't wrong."

Gareth had years of experience to hone his skills of persuasion. He had swayed and won over Old Bailey judges and juries as well as his own clients. Just as Gareth suspected, a little praise and vanity stroking put Simon at ease.

"There is one condition. My client wants to be certain

that all your cannons will make it past military inspection."

A smug grin spread across Simon's face. "It's not a problem. I've devised a way."

Gareth studied Simon. "How?"

"Your client wishes to remain anonymous and I wish to keep my secrets. That being said, you can reassure him that the cannons will pass inspection," said Simon.

Sunlight from the window reflected off the cut crystal. Gareth sipped his drink. He knew when to retreat. He didn't want to arouse Simon's suspicions. He'd have to unearth the information another way. For now he had gained some of Marbury's trust. Enough to enter into business together.

Gareth leaned back in his leather chair. "You were at the theatre with Lady Stanwell last night."

"You saw her?" Simon asked.

"I saw you leave together," Gareth lied. Although he hadn't seen Jane and Simon depart the theatre, he wanted to know what happened between them after the play ended.

"Yes, the lovely Jane. It was quite an entertaining evening."

Gareth's muscles immediately tensed. Had Simon taken her to his home? Had they spent the night together?

"I also happened to be pleasantly distracted by a light skirt in the hall," Simon continued. "You never know who you may encounter at the theatre."

Gareth forced himself to relax. Simon referred to Lady Weatherby. It was her job to distract Marbury so Gareth could sneak into the private theatre box and speak with Jane.

Ah, but he'd done more than simply speak with her. Her lips had been warm and moist, and despite pushing him away, he'd felt her shiver in longing and the harsh uneven rhythm of her breathing. It took all his self control not to crush her to him, and her throaty sighs had haunted him all night.

"A light skirt, you say? What about Lady Stanwell?" Gareth asked.

"She's proving to be a bit of a challenge. I had planned to end up in her bed at the end of the night, but I sensed she would refuse. I went to the Seven Sins afterward."

Gareth's relief was palpable. His reaction bothered him more than he wanted to admit. He shouldn't care, dammit.

"I will have her yet," Simon said.

Gareth struggled to keep his mask in place. He wanted to reach across the desk and strangle Simon.

*All in good time.*

"I noticed the tension between you at the park. You believe the young widow is a pretty piece as well, don't you?" Simon asked.

Gareth hesitated. He knew better than to outright lie after the scene in the park, but he didn't like where the topic of conversation was headed.

"She's attractive," Gareth said.

"How about a wager? Who can bed her first?"

"I don't want to bed her," Gareth said. Only now he did lie. He wanted desperately to bed her.

Simon waved his hand dismissively. "We can share her."

"I don't share." Not Jane anyway.

Simon slapped the desk. "Ha! Spoken like a true barrister. You must join us tonight at Vauxhall Gardens. Jane is accompanying me along with a few friends."

Jane was going to Vauxhall with Simon and his dissolute friends? Would she never learn?

"I'll be there."

# Chapter Nine

Jane smoothed her skirts as she sat in the boat across from Simon. "It's been a long time since I've visited Vauxhall Gardens," she said.

Simon chuckled. "Didn't your husband take you?"

"Yes, but only during the day. It's much more exciting after dark."

The boat ride across the Thames to Vauxhall Gardens went swiftly, and soon they passed through the water entrance.

The boatman maneuvered the boat to the quayside. Simon stepped out, then assisted Jane to dry land.

Jane adjusted her evening cloak, which covered an expensive gown of cerulean blue trimmed with silver that boasted a scandalously low neckline. With her fair hair piled high in an elegant style with loose curls brushing her bare shoulders, she knew she looked attractive.

"Will your friends join us?" she asked.

Simon's hair and face looked pale in the moonlight.

"Lord Hartley and Lady Preston will meet us at my private supper box."

Jane knew of Hartley. He was an heir to an earldom and a bachelor. Lady Preston was a dashing widow of a marquess and close to Jane's age. She had been briefly introduced to Lady Preston at a ball years ago when they were both newly married. But unlike Charles, Lady Preston's husband had been much older and had died of natural causes.

"I also invited Mr. Ramsey to join us this evening," Simon said.

Jane took a quick breath. Gareth? Must he be everywhere? She recalled Gareth telling Simon they had business to discuss at the park. Is that why he was part of Simon's group of friends?

She had little time to contemplate her thoughts. They walked the short distance to the entrance, where Simon paid the fee to enter the gardens. He led her down a winding gravel pathway.

Lanterns lit the way. They walked for a while until they turned right and she halted.

Jane gasped. "It's beautiful and looks so different at night!"

Meticulously landscaped gardens illuminated with hundreds of lanterns branched off into intricate private arbors and hedges. Lovely tree-lined promenades and gravel-paths invited leisurely walks by visitors. An orchestra housed in a rotunda played lively music for dancing, and a pavilion with supper boxes served food. In the distance, a dozen lanterns lit Roman inspired ruins and elegant fountains of swans and mermaids. The sound of music, the glow of the lanterns, and the scent of flowering shrubs and greenery wafted to her.

Simon reached for her gloved hand. "Come. I see my friends."

He led her to a supper box big enough to hold eight guests comfortably. Fine crystal and tableware glittered brightly beneath the lanterns, and the walls of the box were decorated with a William Hogarth painting.

Lord Hartley was of medium height and build with pale blue eyes and a balding pate of thinning red hair. He bowed when she entered the box.

"Charmed," Hartley said.

Lady Preston rose from her seat to glide forward. She was an attractive woman with dark hair and tip-tilted green eyes that gave her a sultry appearance. Her emerald gown had an even lower bodice than Jane's that managed to be scandalous and stylish at once. Fat curls crowned her head, and a brilliant cut emerald the size of a walnut glittered in the deep valley between her breasts.

"Welcome to our group," Lady Preston said, then came close to kiss the air on both sides of Jane's cheeks.

At the scrape of booted feet behind her, a prickle of awareness tingled down Jane's spine. She spun around to see a dark figure step from the shadows and enter the supper box.

Gareth.

He was striking in a simple navy jacket and buff waistcoat, and his ruggedly handsome features gave him a predatory look. A wayward lock of dark, curling hair brushed his forehead. She resisted the urge to reach out and smooth it back. There was such a firm strength about him, and he exuded confidence. Standing next to Simon Marbury and Lord Hartley, Gareth's broad shoulders made the others appear like boys.

The men shook hands and Lady Preston curtsied.

Then, at last, Gareth turned to her.

"Lady Stanwell," he said simply.

The glow of a nearby lantern gave his eyes a feral yellow appearance that reminded her of a wolf.

She curtsied, avoiding his gaze. "Mr. Ramsey."

"Let us sit and enjoy the evening," Simon said.

Gathering her senses, Jane looked about frantically, hoping not to sit beside Gareth. The decision was made for her when Simon motioned for her to sit next to him. Lord Hartley occupied her other side.

Soon after, a waiter arrived.

"The arrack punch," Simon said. "We want to mix our own."

They ordered and soon the group began conversing. Jane had difficulty following the conversation. She stole a glimpse at Gareth and was dismayed to find Lady Preston in deep conversation with him. Her heavy lidded green gaze never left his face. She laughed and her bejeweled fingers rose to her low-cut bodice in a clear attempt to draw Gareth's attention to her breasts.

Heat rose in Jane's face at the lady's shocking behavior.

The spirits arrived along with chicken, shaved pieces of ham, and salad.

"The wafer-thin ham is a Vauxhall Gardens favorite," Hartley said. "But the punch is not to be missed."

Simon mixed the punch by adding rum, lemon, arrack, and sugar. A glass was handed to Jane. She raised the glass to her lips and swallowed. The potent alcohol burned her throat, and she sputtered and coughed.

Lady Preston laughed. "Simon's punch is notoriously

potent, but delicious. The more you drink the easier it goes down." The lady raised her glass and waited for Jane to do the same.

Jane caught Gareth's glittering black gaze of disapproval across the table. Clearly he didn't want her drinking. But what right did he have to tell her what to do?

Jane raised her glass and took another sip. The alcohol quickly took effect, warming her blood and easing her nerves.

As the evening progressed, the amount of alcohol that Simon and his friends consumed was shocking. As the punch continued to flow freely, the laughter grew louder and the conversation grew coarser and lewder.

Lady Preston's veiled looks at Gareth became bolder. Her expression was hungry, lustful.

Jane stirred in her seat.

Simon leaned toward her and Lord Hartley. "Lady Stanwell is officially out of mourning."

Hartley raised his glass. "To the living!" His breath smelled of rum.

Simon laughed. "The lady is looking for excitement and pleasure."

Hartley's brow rose. "Truly?"

Jane opened her mouth to protest, then stopped. She'd never intended Simon to tell others of her intentions. But what harm could come of it? Lord Hartley was clearly into his cups. Would he even remember what was said tomorrow?

Simon winked and gripped the back of Jane's chair. It was nearly an embrace. "I promised the lady I'd help her."

"I envy you, Marbury," Hartley slurred.

Out of the corner of her eye, she saw Lady Preston lean close to Gareth. Her lips grazed his ear as she whispered, and her finger trailed down his chest. Seconds later, Gareth grinned.

Jane's blood pounded. She reached for her glass. She knew the alcohol was affecting her. She knew and she didn't care. Jane turned her attention to flirting outrageously with Simon and Hartley.

Gareth Ramsey could go to the devil!

• • •

The evening was not progressing the way Gareth had expected. He'd planned to get closer to Simon Marbury, to cultivate the fragile trust between them.

And to watch Jane.

Instead he was seated beside Lady Preston. The distance separating him from Jane in the supper box may have been only a few feet, but it seemed much, much farther as he watched her between Marbury and Hartley.

Lady Preston placed her hand on his sleeve. "You are a barrister, correct?"

"I am."

"I've heard of your reputation. They say you obtained a divorce for a member of the *ton.*"

Who hadn't heard? Many society ladies were put off by his reputation. After all, Gareth had proven the adultery of his clients' wives, never the husbands. But clearly Lady Preston was not dismayed.

She licked her full bottom lip. "You are considered ruthless in the courtroom."

"It was one case, Lady Preston," Gareth said.

She tsked. "You must call me Serena. May I tell you a

secret?"

Gareth inclined his head. "If you like."

She leaned close and whispered in his ear. "I prefer big, muscular men. The fiercer in the bedroom the better." Her hand slipped beneath the table to boldly graze his thigh.

There was a time he would have found the lady's brazenness arousing. With her raven hair and voluptuous figure, she was an attractive woman. And the worldly glint in her gaze said she'd know how to please a man in bed. At one point in his life, he would have taken what she offered without a second thought. But tonight he simply found her annoying.

His gaze returned to Jane seated between Marbury and Lord Hartley. She looked achingly beautiful in her deep blue gown, her golden hair gleaming. The glow from the dozens of lanterns made her skin appear as smooth and pale as the pearls adorning her ears.

Simon's eyes traveled over Jane with unmistakable lust. Hartley's gaze fell to the creamy expanse of Jane's neck, then lower, to the tops of her breasts above the rounded bodice of her gown. A lascivious gleam lit Hartley's beady eyes.

Jane continued to drink and flirt with the two men. Her face was flushed, and Gareth knew the potent punch was affecting her senses. He was again struck by her innocence. She may pretend to be a sophisticated widow, but her wide-eyed expressions at the men's comments said otherwise.

Did she even know Hartley was drunk, and salivated for her? Did she know of Simon's corrupt sexual practices?

When Hartley reached past Jane to grasp the arrack, purposely stroking the side of Jane's breast, Gareth's blood temperature climbed ominously.

He needed to get Jane out of here.

# Chapter Ten

"Vauxhall Gardens in the evening is wonderful," Jane gushed. "Thank you for bringing me."

"It is merely a start." Simon rose and offered his arm. "Come. The orchestra is playing again. We must dance."

She stood and placed her hand on his sleeve. Leaving the supper box, they proceeded to the rotunda. They were soon surrounded by a throng of others enjoying the entertainment.

Jane felt engulfed. She had drunk three glasses of Simon's punch, and she felt slightly unsteady on her feet. The lanterns began to blur, the laughter and chatter of all the other people echoed around her. They joined the quadrille, and the dancers on either side of her moved gracefully as they formed the figures. Jane concentrated on the steps and was grateful when the dance ended and Simon drew her aside.

"Is this the excitement and fun you've been craving?" Simon asked.

"It's wonderful."

"This is only the beginning. To experience all life has to offer you must share it with friends," Simon said.

"Your friends are very welcoming," Jane said.

Simon flashed a white smile. "Hartley likes you."

Hartley? What was he saying? She squinted and tried to focus on his features.

"Come home with me tonight, my lady. Let us pleasure you."

Her head spun. She must have misheard him. He couldn't possibly be suggesting…

Her arm was suddenly grasped from behind. She whirled to find Gareth staring down at her.

"The lady promised me this dance," Gareth said.

Lady Preston stood beside Gareth, a look of confusion on her face. Had the two of them been dancing together and Jane hadn't noticed? The lady pouted, looking displeased.

"Let us switch partners." Gareth thrust Lady Preston at Simon, then took Jane's arm.

The dance had changed, and Gareth swung her into a cotillion. She couldn't believe his audacity. She had never promised him a dance and he damn well knew it. Agitated, she lost count of the steps and stumbled.

He was by her side in a flash, grasping her arm once again.

"Come with me," he said.

She had little choice but to follow him. She thought he would lead her back to the supper box, but he steered her down the gravel path past the artificial Roman ruins and statues. The music and chatter faded in the background.

She rushed to keep up with his long strides. "Where are we going?"

He ignored her and turned right, down a pathway lined

with trees and tall hedges. A fountain gurgled somewhere in the distance.

Gareth's face was stark in the moonlight. "Do you have any idea what kind of danger you're exposing yourself to?"

"What danger? I was dancing in Vauxhall Gardens with a very handsome man. You're the one who has an uncontrollable urge to pull me away."

"I'm saving you."

"From what?"

"Little fool! You've been drinking the potent arrack for an hour at Simon's urging. He's purposely adding stronger and stronger spirits to each glass in order to get you drunk and more susceptible to his advances," he said as he pulled her more deeply into the secluded path.

She halted, digging her slippers into the gravel. "You can't be serious."

Tall and built, he towered over her. "You should thank me."

Her incredulity veered sharply to anger. "Thank you! You keep showing up and interfering in my life!"

Gareth glared at her. "You should thank me for that, too."

Her eyes narrowed. "Of all the insolent—" She stopped, knowing her next choice of words would be entirely unladylike. "Your male vanity is wounded just because I chose Simon over you."

"For a widow you are completely naive when it comes to the base needs of men such as Marbury."

Hands on her hips, she met his hard gaze. "Meaning?"

"One more drink and you would find yourself in his home tonight going along with whatever sexual games Marbury concocts. Games in which his friends, including Lord Hartley, can freely participate to enhance Marbury's own enjoyment."

She took a quick, sharp breath. "You're lying. You want me to like you. To choose you to be first on my list."

The look in his eyes was hot and intense. "*Like* is not the word I would use to describe what I want you to feel with me."

A delicious shiver ran down her spine and heated her blood. She thought herself capable of resisting Gareth Ramsey. She feared her defenses were crumbling. Everything about him was titillating, from his rugged features to his broad, muscular chest. Simon's kisses made her feel insipid, whereas Gareth's left her hot and wanting. The desire she'd felt had been heady in his arms. Nothing in her past came close to compare.

"You are supposed to be Simon's friend," she argued.

"We are involved in business matters, but we are not friends," he said.

Questions plagued her, and she fought to ignore the pull between them and hold on to her reason. "You want me to be grateful to you. To consider you instead of him. How am I to be sure you haven't been waiting for me to become intoxicated before dragging me off into the shrubs?"

His eyes blazed with sudden anger, and she feared she had pushed him too far.

"I've never needed to intoxicate a woman to get her to share my bed," he said.

She thought of Lady Preston, who looked at him with lust. She didn't doubt his words. There was something about this man, something dangerously scintillating in his rugged, dark looks that tempted a woman. She was honest enough with herself to admit that Simon's appearance may have initially drawn her eye, but he did not captivate her like Gareth Ramsey.

His words were starting to set in, but still her mind floundered. "Why would Simon need to get a woman foxed when he's so—"

"When he's so very handsome," Gareth said, repeating her earlier words. "I cannot answer that question. I can only tell you that some men take gross pleasure in using and abusing women, demoralizing them."

Could it be true? Simon's cryptic words came back to her in a rush. *To experience all life has to offer you must share it with friends. Hartley likes you.*

She shivered, this time in revulsion. She was sheltered when it came to men's sexual urges. Charles had been consumed with his horses, not with the bedroom.

What did she really know of Simon Marbury?

He was the heir to a wealthy industrialist and a sought-after guest by the society hostesses as a gentleman of fashion. He was also a sworn bachelor, but maybe his aversion toward marriage was because of his profligate preferences, and he did indeed have a sinful reputation.

She'd never inquired before. And Olivia, as an unmarried lady, wouldn't have heard all the rumors.

The truth of Gareth's words suddenly struck her, and she looked up at him.

"If what you're saying is true—"

"It is."

"Then why didn't you tell me sooner?"

"Would you have believed me?"

She hesitated. The truth was, she would not have believed him. She would have doubted Gareth's word.

Her bottom lip trembled. "Then I do believe I owe you a debt of gratitude."

Gareth let out a sigh. "You're not going to faint, are you?"

She straightened her shoulders. "I'm made of sterner stuff. I never faint."

"Good." He grasped her hand. "Come with me."

She pulled against him. "But I don't want to return to the group," she protested.

"You're not. At least not for long."

She allowed him to lead her out of the seclusion of the tall hedges. Retracing their steps, they followed the main gravel path to the supper box.

Simon rose from his seat as they approached. "Where have you been?"

Gareth stepped close, effectively preventing Simon from taking Jane's arm. "Be grateful, Marbury. She spent the past half hour spewing in the gardens," Gareth said.

Simon's face wrinkled in disgust.

Jane's face heated, but she didn't contradict the statement.

"I'm taking her home," Gareth said.

He didn't wait for a response. Fetching her cloak, he turned and steered her toward the exit.

Jane struggled to keep up. Her vision was spinning now. She should protest; she shouldn't allow him to escort her home.

He was dangerous, unpredictable. He was every inch a dominant male, and she could feel the power that coiled within him as he walked beside her. She ought to be wary and afraid.

So why was her stomach tight with anticipation instead of anxiety? Her heart jolted at the realization that his size and strength no longer intimidated her, but made her feel safe.

They made it to the quayside where a boatman awaited. She halted, grasping her skirts and wondering how on earth she would step into the gently swaying boat when she was already unsteady on dry land.

Her quandary was resolved as Gareth easily picked her up, stepped into the boat, and set her down on the wooden seat across from him.

The boatman pushed off from the quayside.

"You've had too many drinks of punch, my lady," Gareth said.

She didn't argue with him. Instead she met his gaze. "You're not the hard, emotionless barrister you portray to others."

"Meaning?"

"You saved the boy in the park."

"Anyone would—"

"Simon didn't. And your concern for me tonight."

"Again—"

"No." She shook her head. "You're kind-hearted, soft beneath your gruff exterior."

He flashed a crooked smile. "Soft? Now that's an insult."

She tilted her head to the side. "I don't mean it as such."

He placed a finger under her chin and forced her gaze to his. "Don't turn me into a hero, Jane. I stated my intentions quite clearly. I want to be your lover. I want the privilege of showing you how pleasurable it can be between us, how passionate."

She nearly gasped out loud at the raw lust in his eyes. A rush of heat washed over her and spread to her limbs. Gathering her courage, she swallowed and held his stare. "What if I told you I want that, too?"

# Chapter Eleven

Gareth inhaled sharply. Jane looked up at him with doe-like eyes…innocent and temptress at once.

"You're drunk. You don't know what you're saying," he said gruffly.

"I assure you I do," Jane insisted.

"Only moments ago you wanted Marbury, remember?"

"No. I tried to convince myself, but I never felt a spark when Simon kissed me."

Jealousy flared, dark and tumultuous inside him. "When did the bastard kiss you?"

"It no longer matters," she said breathlessly. "I find myself drawn to you. Perhaps it's the punch talking, but it's made me bolder, able to speak the truth."

Reaching out, she touched his cheek…softly, sensuously. He nearly jumped out of his skin.

*Sweet Jesus.*

Her words inflamed him, and her touch aroused him.

The boat came to a stop, and the boatman jumped out and anchored the little craft. Gareth assisted Jane to dry land and into his awaiting carriage. He gave the driver her Piccadilly address.

"Not your address?" she asked boldly.

His tone was hoarse to his own ears. "No."

She leaned against him in the carriage. Locks of blond hair had escaped her topknot and caressed her high cheekbones and tops of her shoulders. Her eyes fluttered closed and he thought she would doze, He inhaled her tantalizing fragrance of faint summer lilacs. She nestled against him, her soft curves molding to him.

When he shifted, she opened her eyes, and tipped her face to his.

Just one taste of her lips.

Just one.

It took very little pressure to draw her fully into his arms. His lips claimed hers, searing and passionate. He sucked her plump lower lip into his mouth and she made moaning noises that ratcheted his desire. He tried to pull away, but she didn't let him. Reaching up, she grasped the back of his head and thrust her tongue into his mouth.

She would drive him completely mad. She tasted of arrack and strawberries and he knew one kiss wasn't enough. His body grew taut and heavy with lust. His tightly leashed control snapped; his reason fled.

He pushed aside her cloak and cupped her full breasts. His thumbs traced hardening nipples through the blue satin, and she gasped and pulled him closer, urging him on. A bead of sweat formed on his brow. It would be so easy to lower her to the carriage seat, lift her skirts, and bury himself deeply inside her.

She was eager and willing.

And very intoxicated.

A gentleman would escort her safely to her door, thrust her into her housekeeper's arms, and leave.

But he had never been a gentleman, had he? It didn't matter that he was the younger son of a baron; he'd never acted the part. And more often his employment as a barrister had been a foil for his covert activities for the Home Office. Espionage was his true calling. Deception and trickery had become second nature.

But this was Jane. And she deserved better than a quick toss of her skirts in the back of a carriage.

With a ragged breath, he drew his hands away from her. Wiping his brow, he said, "This isn't a good idea."

She stiffened. "You're worried about complications, aren't you?"

He couldn't answer. Looking into her brown eyes, he detected no deception, only innocence, and heaven help him, trust.

She trusted *him.*

She should be wary of him. If she knew all his past sins, she would surely flee. It didn't matter that they were carried out for King and Country. He'd used people, destroyed their lives, and not all had been guilty of treason.

Yet there was no mistaking the emotion shining in Jane's eyes.

"You needn't worry, Gareth. I don't want a commitment or a relationship from you. There will be other men in my future," she said matter-of-factly.

His muscles clenched. He didn't like the thought of other men in Jane's life let alone her bed. He wanted to be her *sole* lover.

Now where did that notion come from?

He'd never been a jealous man or had a problem leaving a woman. He'd preferred it simple.

No emotional bindings. No hysterical women, no tears.

But now the thought of another man in Jane's life made him want to hit something. She was inebriated, he reminded himself, she had no idea what she was saying.

"It's still not a good idea. You're—"

She grasped his sleeve, her full breasts rising and falling in her low bodice. "You don't have to worry about pregnancy either. I'm barren, you see."

Once again, she took him off guard. "That's not what—"

She leaned closer, her magnificent breasts pressing against his arm. "There's no risk. We can share a passionate night and pretend ignorance tomorrow," she said breathlessly.

His cock jerked in excitement. But something was wrong about what she offered—wrong in a way he'd never before experienced. He stared at her kiss-swollen lips and her eyes smoky with awakened passion, and cursed.

"You're drunk," he said again, more gruffly this time.

"So? For the first time in my life, I know what I want."

And she wanted him.

His trousers stretched tighter, a feat he'd thought impossible. But would she regret it in the morning? When the alcohol burned away, would she bury her face in her pillow in shame, or worse, hate him for taking advantage?

He'd never cared in the past. He'd only sought lovers for a night. But now he wanted more.

The carriage stopped before a red brick town house. The footman lowered the step, and Gareth helped her from the carriage. She leaned on him as they climbed the steps of her porch.

"If you won't take me to your home, will you come inside?" Her lips grazed his throat, soft, wet, inviting. She clung to his arm, those lush breasts still pressing against him.

Gareth clenched his jaw with iron control. He leaned her against the side of the town house, held her by the waist to keep her pinned against the wall, and banged on the door with his other fist.

"What are you doing?" she asked in alarm.

"Damned if I know," he ground out.

After a long minute of Jane pressed against him, Gareth started to doubt his sanity. "Where's your butler," he growled.

"Graves is in his eighties and has trouble hear—"

Gareth banged on the door, louder this time. He was surprised the neighbors didn't come running.

At last the door opened. An old man appeared dressed in black and white servant's garb with tufts of gray hair and thick spectacles. The butler's face was incredulous as he looked at Gareth, then at Jane held up against the red brick.

"Lady Stanwell?" the servant asked.

A second later, an elder, plump woman appeared at the door. Her robe was hastily donned over her night rail, and her cap looked like a large mushroom atop her head. He assumed she was the housekeeper.

"See to your mistress," Gareth said, thrusting Jane into the astonished woman's arms.

Turning quickly, he fled to the waiting carriage.

• • •

Gareth had rejected her.

Jane couldn't believe her ill fortune. Stunned, she turned to find Aunt Eleanor and Graves, her butler, staring at her. Concern etched on their features.

Just splendid. She'd woken her elderly household once again. Only this time it wasn't from screams of terror due to another nightmare over Charles.

"What happened?" Eleanor asked.

Jane's voice cracked. "Nothing."

Jane grasped the banister tightly as she climbed the stairs. Eleanor was right beside her with her cane.

"I'll never find a lover," Jane muttered miserably.

"Hush, darling."

Jane rubbed her temple. "He banged on the door and fled."

"Who was he?"

"Mr. Gareth Ramsey. He rejected me."

"Hmmm. As you're clearly foxed, he seems like a perfect gentleman to me."

They reached the top of the landing. "That's what I told him earlier, but he denied it."

Eleanor opened Jane's bedroom door and led her inside. "Denied what? That you're foxed?"

"No, that he's really a gentleman beneath his rough façade," Jane said.

Jane's maid entered the room, efficiently unhooked her mistress's dress, and helped her into her nightgown and beneath the covers before quietly leaving. Aunt Eleanor remained.

"You need sleep," Eleanor said.

Jane yawned. "He doesn't want me."

"I don't think that's the case. Not by the look of him. I'd say you have him wound up like a top and you won't have to wait long to see him again."

Jane blinked and focused on her aunt. "Really? You truly think so?"

Eleanor chuckled. "I was married to your uncle, remember? I can recognize desire in a man."

Jane yawned. Her lids felt very heavy and she pulled the coverlet up to her chin. "I hope you're right. Or perhaps this whole evening is a nightmare that I will awake from tomorrow morning."

• • •

After dropping Jane off, Gareth directed his driver to Daniel Forster's town house on St. James's street.

Daniel's butler didn't blink an eye to find Gareth on the porch well past midnight. The servant was accustomed to the unconventional hours of Daniel's espionage activities and acquaintances.

Daniel turned the corner into the vestibule and halted when he spotted Gareth. "You look like hell. What happened to you?"

Gareth handed his cloak and hat to the butler. "Nothing."

"Then why are you here?"

"Can't a friend drop by for a drink?"

Daniel eyed him strangely. "Aren't you supposed to be entertaining Simon Marbury tonight?"

"I was, but there was an unforeseeable complication."

Daniel motioned down the corridor. "I was in the study."

Gareth followed Daniel down the hall and into the study. Daniel closed the door behind them. Two lamps burned brightly on a large oak desk. Rows of bookshelves holding colorful leather bound volumes lined the walls, and a globe rested on an end table in the corner of the room.

Daniel went to a sideboard, poured two glasses of whiskey, and handed one to Gareth. "Tell me what happened."

Gareth took a swallow before answering. "Simon arrived with Lady Stanwell and his friends at Vauxhall Gardens. They proceeded to get drunk."

Daniel shrugged. "So?"

Gareth stared at the remaining whiskey in his glass. "Jane became intoxicated and was to be their entertainment for the evening. I had no choice but to take her home before she was violated."

Daniel sipped from his glass and regarded him. "You're not supposed to warn Lady Stanwell away from Simon Marbury. You're supposed to get close to Marbury by whatever means necessary, even if that means using the lady to do so."

"I know," Gareth growled. "I just couldn't allow Marbury to drug and rape Jane."

"You care for the lady, don't you?" Daniel said.

Gareth's gut tightened. He didn't like where the conversation was heading. "Care for her? I don't care for any woman."

"Your actions suggest differently."

Daniel could be relentless in his questioning. Gareth knew his friend's ability was one of the reasons he'd been appointed as undersecretary of the Home Office. At other times Gareth had admired the trait, but not when Daniel used his talent on him.

Gareth drained his glass in one gulp. "I desire her. I want to bed her. Is that what you want to hear?" He knew he sounded surly.

"You still could have bedded her after Simon had his

fun with her tonight," Daniel said.

"Don't talk about her that way," Gareth snapped.

A log crackled in the hearth. Several seconds passed before Daniel spoke. "Our work is never easy, Gareth. It takes a high emotional toll. Even Robert wasn't immune, remember?"

Robert Ware, the earl of Kirkland, had been the first to be recruited by the Home Office and first to marry. No one thought Robert would remarry after his first wife had been murdered, but he'd surprised them all.

"My actions tonight have nothing in common with Robert's past," Gareth said.

Daniel shrugged. "I can assign your mission to another."

"No." The denial came out quickly and revealed more than Gareth intended. He cursed himself silently at Daniel's knowing look. Gareth ran his hand through his hair and let out a breath. "I'm perfectly capable of completing the mission. Besides, Marbury trusts me and we are already business partners. He'd never work with another now."

Daniel placed his whiskey on the mantle and casually leaned against the back of a leather chair. "Still, I understand if your feelings for Lady Stanwell are getting in the way…"

Gareth's cravat felt tight as a noose, and perspiration beaded on his brow. He knew Daniel was manipulating him and he should tell him to sod off, but he didn't want to give him the satisfaction. "I don't love her, if that's what you're suggesting. Lust isn't love."

He was convinced once he bedded Jane he would no longer think about her. He'd never had a problem forgetting about a woman before. Commitment made him uneasy, and he had no desire to converse with a woman other than how best to remove her clothing in the bedchamber. He knew he was jaded when it came to the female sex and the notion of love. He didn't even believe in the emotion. Countless disgruntled men came to his Gray's Inn chambers seeking his aid. He'd made a living listening to their marital problems and how love had been an illusion that had deserted them.

As for his unexplainable and maddening attraction to Jane, it was the challenge, the chase. It couldn't be anything more for him.

"I never mentioned love," Daniel said simply.

"Then what?"

"I've known you since our school days, Gareth. I've never seen you agitated over a woman."

Gareth clenched his fist and shot Daniel a withering glare. "I'm not agitated."

He wasn't, was he? He never let women get under his skin.

But Jane was different.

There was more to her. She'd been betrayed by her husband, but she was a survivor. As for Simon Marbury, she had no idea of the man's criminal activities. She didn't know about the inferior cannons. She had no idea Private Stevens was lying in a hospital bed with his leg blown off, worried about how he would be able to support his wife and newborn child.

Jane was innocent. As innocent as the wounded and dead soldiers from Simon's cannons. Gareth felt overwhelming lust for her yes…but he also admired her for surviving her own tragedy. And even more disturbing, he genuinely liked her.

A wry grimace thinned his lips. "I'll be fine."

Daniel regarded him closely "I've known you a long time, Gareth. Resisting the lady may not be as easy as you think."

# Chapter Twelve

Jane woke the following morning with a pounding headache. She felt as if her head was in a vise, and her mouth was as dry as sandpaper.

She dressed with the help of her maid and made her way to the dining room. She was sipping a cup of hot coffee when Graves announced she had a gentleman caller.

"I put him in the parlor, my lady," Graves said as he held out a silver salver to reveal an embossed calling card resting upon it.

Her heart pounded as she reached for the card.

Simon? Or Gareth?

It must be one of the two.

She hoped it wasn't Simon Marbury. After all, what could she say to him after what she'd learned last night?

Her heart pounded as she read the name on the calling card and realized Gareth was here. Memories of the prior evening rose in her mind. She'd wantonly thrown herself at him, and he'd responded by unceremoniously banging on her front door and thrusting her into her aunt's arms.

Goodness! How could she face him today? She took several deep breaths and gathered her courage before confronting her caller.

Gareth was staring out the window overlooking the street when she entered the parlor. He turned when she closed the door.

He looked fierce and broodingly handsome dressed in a moss colored coat, buff trousers, and gleaming Hessians, and she wondered why she had ever paid any attention to Simon Marbury at all.

Gareth strode over to her side, instantly making her pulse leap. "I came to check on you," he said. "Are you well?"

Jane rubbed her temple. "As well as can be expected," she said with a small smile.

He flashed a crooked smile. "Ah, the effects of too much drink."

"Is that the only reason you're here?" A small part of her wanted his visit to be more than social decorum dictated.

He took a step closer. "I was concerned."

His nearness kindled feelings of fire. "I was unsure if I'd ever see you again."

"I find I cannot stay away from you."

Her heart did a little jump at his words. "I thought I had somehow scared you off by my unladylike behavior."

"You mean your offer to become lovers?"

She flushed. She hadn't expected him to ask her such a forthright question. She smoothed imaginary wrinkles from her skirt. "Well…yes."

He took her hand and led her to a settee.

"Tell me, Jane. Why are you so intent on finding a lover?"

If she had a mirror, she suspected her complexion would be beet red. She'd never anticipated answering such a question by a man when she'd written her list of eligible lovers. She didn't want to answer, but Gareth sat beside her, his gaze unwavering.

She clutched her hands in her lap. "Many widows have affairs and society turns a blind eye."

"Yes, but you're not just any widow."

"Would you ask me such a question if I were a man?" she said.

"Most assuredly, no."

The unfairness of his answer made her spine stiffen. "Then why ask me?"

"Because you are not a man, and you are not a woman who is accustomed to taking lovers."

"How can you assume that?"

"I just know. Even though you were married for years, you are innocent."

The maddening hint of arrogance in his voice was irritating. "I'm hardly a virgin."

"Tell me about your husband," he said.

She was taken aback by the change of topic. "You must know what everyone says. Charles shot himself after his prized stallion lost a race."

"I'm not interested in public knowledge. I want you to tell me about your marriage."

"I'd rather not," she said tensely.

"I need to know, Jane. Did he abuse you?"

She started. She didn't want to think of her unhappy marriage. Not here. Not now. Not with him.

"You can tell me," he urged, softly this time.

Could she? Once again she was struck by how much she trusted Gareth. Was she a fool, or could he truly be the exception to her steadfast rule?

She took a deep breath. "Charles never struck me, if that's what you mean. He was always at the track. He loved his horses, loved the excitement of the race. It was like…like a fever that overtook him and raged inside him."

"He was an addict," Gareth said.

The words came to her easier now. "I tried to keep him from the track, tried so hard to get him to stop, but I couldn't." Her voice choked.

"Neglect is a form of abuse, Jane."

She looked at him in surprise. Did he think so? No one had ever taken her side, except for Olivia. They'd all thought her lacking as a wife. Why else would Charles prefer the track to her bed? It had been humiliating. On more than one occasion, he'd resisted her efforts at seduction only to squirrel himself in his study to analyze sheets and sheets of horse racing statistics.

She'd obviously failed to satisfy her husband in bed. She'd felt completely inadequate as a woman.

Gareth's dark eyes were intent. "Listen to me. It wasn't your fault. Gamblers are like opium addicts. They crave it, need it, and they can't see the warning signs no matter how heavily they lose. They live for the thrill of the next hand of cards, or the next race. It is an illness. No amount of pleading, begging, or bargaining can stop it. No matter how much you love them or how hard you try."

His words, even though softly delivered, spoke volumes. The flicker of emotion in his eyes was unmistakable.

*Hurt. Betrayal.*

"Are you a gambler?" she asked.

He hesitated so long she feared he wouldn't answer.

"No," he finally said. "But my father is."

There was so much more to Gareth Ramsey than she'd initially believed. He'd suffered as well. She imagined him as a young boy craving his father's attention, only to be disappointed time and time again when his parent chose the gaming hells over his young son. She'd heard rumors Gareth was estranged from the baron, and she'd thought they were over his choice of profession.

But she'd been wrong about him.

Again.

"I'm sorry," she said softly.

"Don't be. I've fared well over the years."

He was a successful barrister, a younger son who was no longer dependent on his father for every shilling. She admired him for achieving financial independence when so many gentlemen of the *ton* thought trade and work beneath them.

"You still haven't explained your ridiculous need to find a lover, starting with your blasted list," he said.

"You're right in that I may not be the most knowledgeable when it comes to taking a lover. All my life I've done what's been expected of me. I was a dutiful daughter of an earl and married my family's choice. I was a dutiful wife. But now—as a widow—I'm finally free to make my own choices. Is there anything wrong in wanting to experience the passion and desire I've missed in my marriage?"

His eyes never left hers for an instant. "No," he said gruffly.

"Then does my offer from last night completely disinterest you?" She tilted her head to the side and regarded him. "Or have you changed your mind about pursuing me?"

A strange, faintly eager look flashed in his eyes. "Hardly. You should know I came very close to directing my driver to my home, sweeping you into my arms, and ravishing you in my bed."

Her mouth gaped at the images his words evoked. "You did?"

"I thought of little else all night."

"Then why didn't you?"

"Because you were foxed! I didn't want you to wake in the morning and have regrets. Worse, I didn't want you to despise me for it."

She froze. He cared for her. He must. As for herself, she could never despise him. She'd come to admire him... to desire him.

Would Simon Marbury have taken such care? Never. He wanted her drunk and unable to defend herself. She shivered at how close she had come to just such a fate.

If not for Gareth's intervention.

"I suppose I should thank you. Again."

He grunted.

"But Gareth?"

"Yes."

"I'm not inebriated now," she pointed out.

"And?"

She scooted toward him on the settee and boldly touched his cheek. He was warm and strong beneath her fingertips, and the tantalizing scent of his shaving soap heightened her senses. "And nothing has changed. I still want what I was able to voice last night," she whispered.

She was enthralled by the primal lust that glittered in his eyes.

"Think about what you're offering, Jane." He took her hand from his cheek and placed a hot kiss in the center of her palm. A tingling began low in her belly.

"I have," she breathed.

He lowered her hand, his fingers entwining with hers. "I cannot believe I'm saying this, but you must be aware that there are consequences."

He held himself rigidly, and she had the impression of a wild tiger stalking its prey, ready to pounce.

"I told you I'm barren. I was never able to have children during my marriage. A doctor confirmed it."

"That's not what I'm talking about. There are other consequences. Emotional ones."

Despite the butterflies in her stomach, she attempted a confident smile. "You needn't fear, Gareth. I won't demand more from you than what lovers share."

His eyes raked boldly over her, and the heated tingling spread to the tips of her breasts.

"Then come to me tonight. I'll send a carriage for you under cover of darkness," he said.

A disturbing thought occurred to her. "Are you worried about being seen with me?"

"Society can go to the devil! It's not my reputation I'm concerned about, but yours as a lady."

"I see."

"Knock on the servants' quarters. I'll be waiting." He came close and fingered a loose tendril of hair on her cheek. "But know this. I want you very much. If your servants weren't close by, I would lay you down on this settee, remove your pretty gown, and show you how much."

Her knees felt weak and she was grateful she was sitting. "But Jane—"

"Yes?"

"Be certain."

• • •

Jane needed to speak with Olivia, but when she arrived at the Newbury's home she was informed by the butler that Lady Olivia and her mother were at the milliners. Jane headed straight to Bond Street in search of her friend.

Olivia waved as Jane entered the shop. "Jane! Are you shopping for a new bonnet?"

Jane wove through the shop to where Olivia stood and grasped her friend's hand. "I need to speak with you privately," she said in a low voice.

Olivia's brows rose to her hairline at the urgency in Jane's voice. Her eyes darted to where her mother, Lady Newbury, was inspecting ribbons at a far off table. "Of course. Mother's preoccupied at the moment. Let's go in the back."

Under pretense of comparing lace on bonnets, they disappeared around a tall shelf.

"I've arranged a rendezvous for tonight," Jane whispered.

Olivia looked at her expectantly. "You're meeting Mr. Marbury?"

"No, not Simon."

"Then who?"

"Mr. Gareth Ramsey."

Olivia dropped the bonnet in her hands. "Oh my."

"Are you shocked?" Jane asked.

"Yes, but relieved as well. I never thought Mr. Marbury was meant for you. He is too conceited, and frankly, there's something about him that's just cold."

Jane glanced from side to side to ensure shoppers had not wandered close, and then lowered her voice even further. "Your instincts were right. Simon planned to get me intoxicated in Vauxhall Gardens and for me to join both him and Lord Hartley in his home for their depravity."

Olivia gasped. "You're serious?"

Jane swallowed the lump in her throat and nodded. "Gareth intervened and escorted me safely home."

"Thank goodness! Mr. Ramsey's clearly taken with you."

Jane recalled Gareth earlier that morning. She'd never forget the look of raw lust in his eyes when he'd admitted that he'd thought of her all evening. She experienced a swooping pull low in her belly.

"I'm to meet him under cover of darkness tonight," Jane said.

Olivia clasped her hand. "How exciting! Are you nervous?"

She hadn't much time for anxiety to set in. Last night had been a blur. This morning her head had ached, and before she could drink her morning cup of coffee, Gareth had arrived. But now, hours later, standing in the milliner's shop, her stomach did flutter with anticipation and nerves.

"I suppose so," Jane said. "I may have been intimate with Charles, but he had always been…how can I phrase it… quick about coupling." Her face was surely red.

"Do you trust Mr. Ramsey?"

"Yes," she said without hesitation.

Olivia sucked in a breath. "I never thought you'd trust

another man after Charles's death."

"Shocking, isn't it?"

Olivia smiled and picked up a bonnet with yellow silk flowers and ribbon from a nearby shelf. "I'm glad. And you shouldn't worry about your experience. You certainly have more knowledge than me. I've never been alone with Edward for more than an hour. I fear I'll disappoint him with my ignorance on our wedding night."

"Nonsense. You're expected to be a virgin. I, on the other hand, am supposed to be a worldly widow seeking a lover."

Olivia clenched the bonnet in her hands. Surely the ribbon would be wrinkled.

"I have a secret of my own," Olivia whispered.

For the first time that morning, Jane noticed Olivia's appearance. Faint, blue circles were under her eyes, and her normally immaculate topknot was slightly unruly. Guilt assailed Jane. She'd been so consumed with her own affairs she hadn't thought of her best friend.

"What's amiss, Olivia?"

Olivia glanced around a tall shelf to make certain her mother was still occupied comparing ribbons. "Edward's having troubles with a gambling debt."

Jane froze. "I didn't know the duke gambled."

Olivia shrugged a dainty shoulder, but Jane suspected her friend wasn't as undisturbed as she wanted to portray. "He doesn't, not anymore than what's expected of a gentleman attending his clubs. But his brother, William, does."

Jane knew William. Edward's twin, who was second born, had a reputation of dissoluteness and recklessness.

"William doesn't have the responsibility of the dukedom hanging around his neck, and he's certainly not being hounded by the dowager to produce an heir," Olivia said.

"I take it William is in trouble?" Jane said.

"He's a spendthrift. His monthly allowance is quite generous, but even so, it's gone by the middle of the month. According to Edward, William borrowed money from a moneylender and his loan is past due. William is begging Edward to pay off the loan."

"Will he do it?"

Olivia shook her head and thrust the bonnet back on the shelf. Several yellow silk petals bent beyond repair. "Edward would never allow his brother to be harmed. He also wants to keep it secret from the dowager. But I can't help but be concerned," she said in a dull and troubled voice.

"Why?"

Two deep lines of worry appeared between Olivia's eyes. "Edward frets that his assistance has allowed his brother to continue on this dangerous path, and I tend to agree with him. But he is more concerned than usual this time, and I fear something is amiss. Something he's not telling me."

"You must trust Edward's judgment. He's not a fool or a man who acts recklessly," Jane pointed out.

Olivia blinked. "Yes, it's true. Edward is always sensible and responsible."

"Please do not worry for naught, Olivia. Your wedding is little over a month away. Let us focus on more pleasant matters today."

Olivia managed a smile. "You're right, of course. What could be more exciting than bonnets and illicit affairs?"

# Chapter Thirteen

The hood of Jane's cloak covered her fair hair and shadowed her face as she discretely left her home late that night. The doors of the carriage that waited displayed no fancy crest, but as she stepped inside the conveyance, she discovered it to be quite luxurious.

Her composure was a fragile shell as she leaned back on the leather squabs. With a jingle of harness, the horses set off at a brisk pace.

Minutes later, the carriage stopped before an elegant town home. The driver opened the door and lowered the step. "He's waiting for you by the back door, my lady."

She felt her face color. Did the servant know her intent? Was it a common occurrence to have women delivered to Gareth Ramsey's back door step well past midnight?

*There's no turning back now.*

She alighted and made her way along a stone path to the servants' quarters at the back of the house.

She raised a trembling hand to knock just as the door swung open.

Gareth stood in the doorway dressed in a simple white shirt and buff breeches. The interior was dim, and moonlight partly illuminated his strong features.

"Jane," he said as he opened the door wide for her to enter.

She stepped inside a kitchen. In the faint light, she could make out racks of pots and pans hanging from the ceiling and the large shape of an oven. The faint aroma of roast lamb filled the space.

He shut the door and pulled her into his arms. "I thought you wouldn't come."

She felt breathless in response to the warmth and hardness of his body. She raised her face to his. "I said I would."

He pushed back the hood of her cloak. "I've given the servants the evening off. No one will disturb us and your identity will be kept secret. Who knows you're here?"

"Only Lady Olivia. My secret is safe with her."

"Come." He took her hand and led her into the house and up the stairs. She stole a glance at his face. His profile was strong and rigid, and a strange, eager look flashed in his eyes. Her gaze swept from his broad chest to his narrow hips, and a familiar shiver of awareness rippled through her.

She saw no servants as they went, and she was glad he had dismissed them. Her identity would indeed be kept secret.

Then all thought fled as they entered his bedchamber. A low lamp burned, and a large four poster dominated the space. The rest of the furniture—a chest of drawers, a nightstand, two large bookshelves, and a pair of matching leather chairs situated before a large fireplace—were dark mahogany and very masculine. A cheval glass mirror rested in a corner beside the nightstand. A fire burned low in the grate, the flames casting shadows across the room.

"May I take your cloak?" He reached for the tie that fastened the garment and swept it off her shoulders.

She wore the same scarlet gown she had worn the night of the masquerade—the night he'd learned of her list of lovers and when he'd first kissed her. His eyes smoldered as his gaze licked over her, moving leisurely from eyes to mouth to upthrust breasts at her low bodice. An undeniable magnetism built between them, and excitement and a trickle of fear ran down her spine at the knowledge that such a physically powerful male was so anxious to be with her.

He motioned to the corner by the fireplace, and his voice broke the tension. "I had Cook prepare us some food in case you were hungry."

She followed his gaze and noticed a small table tucked in the corner. Upon the snowy linen was a tray laden with an assortment of cheese and fruit. A thoughtful gesture, but she didn't think she could eat even a scrap of bread.

"No, thank you," she said.

"Wine then?"

She nodded. He poured two glasses of wine and handed her a goblet.

"To us," he said, raising his glass.

She obediently drank. The wine was sweet and went down smoothly. Her eyes were once again drawn to the large bed, and she was suddenly assailed by nerves. Her only experience in the bedroom had been with Charles, and he'd expected her to lie on her back and not participate. He hadn't hurt her other than the first time, but neither had he been interested in her pleasure.

She drank more wine. She wouldn't think of Charles.

Not tonight. Not with Gareth.

He must have sensed her anxiety, for he plucked the wine glass from her fingers, set the two glasses on an end table, and placed his hands on her shoulders. "Don't think of the past. Tonight is about you and me. As much as I desire you, I won't rush our intimacy. We have all night."

A shiver ran through her. "I don't want to think of the past, but what if…what if I'm frigid?"

"Impossible. You're too responsive, too passionate to even think such thoughts." He stroked a finger down her cheek. "Nothing but pleasure awaits you in my bed."

The images his words evoked were arousing, but doubts crept into her mind. She searched his face, looking for reassurance. "I was expected to lie still while my husband… while he…"

"Your husband was selfish. That will never happen between us. I long to make your body tremble."

*Oh, my.* "I want that, too."

His gaze was soft as a caress. "Then kiss me, Jane. Show me you want me, that you want this."

Her heart jolted, and her pulse pounded. She came close, rose on tip toe, and touched her lips to his. She was acutely aware of his large body, of the heat emanating from him, and of the faint scent of his shaving soap. She brushed his lips once, twice, then ran her tongue across his full, bottom lip.

He came alive and pulled her fully against his hard length. He kissed her, a long shivery kiss that promised pleasure and ecstasy. A kiss meant to drain away all her doubts and fears.

His hands lifted to remove the pins from her hair, and it tumbled to her shoulders. "Your hair is a golden cloud. I've always wanted to touch it."

He buried his fingers in the silken mass, then lifted a curl to his nose and inhaled her scent. He pushed her hair aside from her nape and pressed his lips to the rapidly beating pulse at her neck. She tilted her head to the side to feel more of his lips and the sweep of his tongue on her nape. Then his tongue grazed the sensitive shell of her ear and sucked the lobe in his hot mouth.

"Does this feel good?"

"Oh, yes," she whispered.

Her heartbeat quickened as she felt his nimble fingers undo the fastenings of her gown. Silk and lace gave way, and her chemise gaped open. His large hands cupped her breasts and his thumbs grazed her nipples, turning them pebble hard. His mouth followed, kissing the top of her left breast, then her right. Exquisite pleasure coursed through her limbs like molten fire, heating them. Every nerve ending was aflame with arousal.

She'd originally believed such a powerful male would dominate his lover to satisfy his desires, but the realization that Gareth was more interested in her pleasure sent a thrill through her.

The gown loosened and slid sinuously down her body to pool at her feet. Her chemise, drawers, and silk stockings did little to shield her from his heated gaze. He picked her up and carried her not to the bed but to the leather chair by the hearth and set her on his lap.

"Do you have any idea how beautiful you are? How much I want you?"

During her marriage, she'd never thought her body desirable to a man. But now, looking into the stark hunger in Gareth's eyes, she felt like a siren.

She wanted this, needed it, craved it with a ferocity equal to his.

"Touch me more," she said. "Touch me *everywhere.*"

He was eager to oblige. His hand trailed down her stomach, caressed the curve of her hip, and lowered to raise the hem of her chemise. His strong fingers caressed her stocking clad leg, up to her frilly garter, and then parted her drawers.

His fingers delved inside her sheath and she groaned out loud, a foreign sound she'd never heard herself make before. Her body ached for his touch, and her pulse skipped wildly. His knowing fingers stroked, then delved, then sinuously slid across a sensitive nub. She panted and wantonly parted her legs to the erotic sensations coursing through her body. She never dreamed she could feel such rapt pleasure. Nothing she'd experienced in her marriage bed could compare, and she knew this was the way intimacy should be between a man and a woman. She writhed beneath him, arched her hips in wanton abandon. Then he lowered his head to lave a nipple and sucked it full into his mouth.

She was close to some cataclysmal event and she instinctively knew that his skillful fingers could give her body what it had never experienced before but craved so desperately. He kissed her just as her scream erupted. Shivers of delight flooded her limbs until she collapsed against him. She buried her face against his throat as her heart rate slowed, and she breathed lightly between parted lips.

Lifting her head, she looked up at him in wonder. "So that's what all the fuss is about? I never knew."

He chuckled, but there was a ferocious hunger in his eyes. She was sprawled across his lap, half undressed, while he was fully clothed. The thought struck her that he'd denied himself pleasure just to ensure hers.

But not without cost to him. His look was so hungry it sent a tremor through her.

Her pulse quickened again, and she had a sudden need to touch him. With trembling fingers she unbuttoned his shirt and thrust her hands inside.

A sprinkling of hair covered his chest and muscles rippled beneath her fingers. She flattened her palms against his skin, and the warmth of his hard flesh was intoxicating. The contrast between her soft curves and the hard planes of his body was shocking and arousing at once.

She squirmed in his lap, felt the hard length of his arousal against her bottom. Would that be as large as the rest of him?

She was no longer afraid, only wildly curious and eager to see him…to touch and stroke his flesh.

He rose swiftly from the chair with her in his arms. "If you have second thoughts, tell me now. I don't think I'll be able to restrain myself once you're in my bed."

Second thoughts? Her body ached anew for his touch.

She cupped his face in her hands. "Show me what I've been missing all these years, Gareth."

With a deep groan, he laid her down on the bed and spread her fair hair around her. He stepped back to jerk his shirt off and toss it carelessly to the floor.

She leaned up on her elbows, eager to see him. Excitement coursed through her at the sight of his broad shoulders and powerful biceps gleaming in the candlelight. Her gaze lowered to the corrugated muscles of his abdomen, then lower still, to a trail of hair that ran down his stomach and disappeared into the waistband of his breeches. His arousal was evident. He towered before her, a lean man of muscle and sinew. His look was hot and intense.

She sat up and reached for the fastenings at the fall of his breeches. Her fingers trembled as the first button slipped through and the fabric parted slightly.

He hissed. "Careful, Jane. I just may ravish you."

A second button loosened to reveal the vermilion tip of his arousal.

Awed, she touched him.

He jerked and groaned. "I want to go slow, to make everything pleasurable for you."

"I want to touch you, too."

"*Yes.*"

She was fascinated by his arousal and wanted to kiss him. To taste him. She lowered her head an inch.

Suddenly a pounding sounded on the door.

Her breath caught in her throat, and she jerked back. Her eyes flew to Gareth's.

"What the hell!" He fastened his breeches and reached for his shirt just as Jane scrambled to cover herself with her dress.

He strode to the door and cracked it open.

"I apologize for the disturbance, Mr. Ramsey."

Jane recognized the voice of the Gareth's driver who had directed her to the back door.

"What's wrong, Brooks?" Gareth said.

"I was waiting in the carriage outside when a young woman showed up and started knocking on the front door. I told her to go away and that no one was home, but she refused to listen and said it's an urgent matter. She kept knocking and started calling out…and well…she was causing a stir on the street by shouting out Lady Stanwell's name."

Jane jumped off the bed. "It must be Lady Olivia!"

Gareth looked at her questioningly.

"Please. It truly must be urgent," Jane said. "She would never come here otherwise."

Gareth turned to his driver. "You did well. Please see the lady to the parlor. We'll join her shortly."

# Chapter Fourteen

Lust pounded in Gareth's veins as he watched Jane struggle with the hooks of her gown. Her back was as smooth as alabaster, and the curve of a full breast peeked from her gaping chemise. Sexual frustration battled with possessiveness. Her passionate response had told him that her husband may have taken her virginity, but he had never been her lover.

Gareth couldn't think about what Jane was going to do with her mouth only moments ago. He took a deep breath, ran a hand through his hair.

Jane gave up with her hooks and reached for a slipper. "I'm worried for Olivia," she said. "She must be in danger for her to risk coming here."

Gareth went to her and helped with her gown. He focused on the task, tried not to think about the warm, soft flesh beneath his fingers.

Jane turned and met his gaze. "She's my close friend, Gareth."

His breath stopped at the worry in her beautiful brown eyes. He was besotted. There was no other explanation.

"Then let's go see what she needs," he said.

Together they rushed down the stairs and into the parlor.

As soon as Olivia spotted Jane, she cried out and embraced her friend. "Thank goodness I found you!"

Jane grasped Olivia's hands. "What's amiss?"

Olivia's eyes darted to Gareth, then back to Jane. Her mouth opened and closed, and it was obvious she was conflicted by his presence.

"I shall leave," Gareth said.

Jane placed a hand on his sleeve and halted him. "No. It's all right, Olivia. Mr. Ramsey will not repeat a word you say. I trust him."

A thrill of male satisfaction coursed through Gareth.

Jane's statement must have convinced Olivia. The lady started speaking rapidly. "It's Edward. He's in trouble. Remember I told you about his brother's, William's, debts to the moneylender?"

"Yes," Jane said.

Olivia nervously bit her lip. "Edward decided to pay off the moneylender, but he didn't trust William to deliver the money himself. Edward thought he would be tempted to stop at a gambling establishment on his way. So Edward went to pay off the moneylender on his own. He was supposed to send word hours ago, but he hasn't. What if he's been hurt?" she said in a choked voice.

Jane tried to comfort her friend. "No, don't think that. Maybe Edward went to his club or to visit friends before—"

"No! He told me he'd deliver a message as soon as he returned. He wouldn't forget." Olivia wrung her hands in her skirts.

Gareth led the overwrought lady to a sofa and sat beside her. He hated female tears, and from the look on Olivia's face, he feared she was about to burst into hysterics.

He spoke in a calm, firm voice. "I will search for the duke, Lady Olivia."

She raised teary eyes to him. "You'd do that?"

Gareth withdrew a handkerchief from his jacket pocket and handed it to her. "Yes. But I need information from you. Do you remember the name of the moneylender?"

Olivia's brow knit as she dabbed at her eyes. "I don't know his true name, but I overheard William tell Edward that the man goes by the name of Snake. I thought it ridiculous at the time."

Gareth's insides went cold. Snake was a ruthless moneylender whose tactics were not only unethical, but barbaric. Gareth had represented a client for legal separation who had dealt with the moneylender once in his past. The man was missing a thumb, Snake's retribution for an unpaid debt.

"One more question. Does William look like Edward?" Gareth asked.

Olivia sniffed. "They are twins. Edward was born ten minutes earlier." Sudden realization dawned on Olivia. "You don't think the moneylender mistook Edward for William, do you?"

It was likely, but he'd never admit it. "You shouldn't fret needlessly," Gareth said. "Men like Snake only want their money. They do not care who pays it."

"Do you know how to find the moneylender?" Olivia asked.

"I have a good idea," Gareth said.

Jane touched his shoulder. "We can accompany you."

Over his dead body. Snake's lair was in a seedy area of St. Giles, certainly no place for two women.

"No," he said, his voice gruffer than he intended. "It's best if I go alone. I'll have my driver escort you both to your homes. I promise to send word as soon as I hear," he said.

Olivia threw herself into his arms. "Thank you, Mr. Ramsey!"

Jane watched him, a strange look in her eyes. She was too intelligent not to see past his vague explanation and must know he was headed for dangerous parts of London.

Could she possibly be concerned for him? No one had expressed concern for his well being—other than Daniel and Robert during a mission—in a long, long time. Certainly not his father, the baron.

A foreign emotion pierced Gareth's chest. He wanted to reassure Jane he could take care of himself and that was an oddity in itself. She was confusing him. Making him weak. He resisted the lure. He refused to allow one night of almost sex to turn him into an infatuated fool.

· · ·

That night Jane found it impossible to sleep. She paced in her bedchamber waiting to hear from Gareth. His driver had dropped her off hours ago. She'd wanted to stay with Olivia, but her friend had sneaked out of the house unchaperoned and both women knew it was best if they returned to their own homes until the morning.

The sun was struggling to rise. Early morning fog curled around distant church spires, and a church bell rang.

Had Gareth found the moneylender? Had he located the duke?

And heaven help her, was Gareth safe?

Her mind turned to the previous night, before Olivia had arrived with her urgent need of help.

Gareth had promised her pleasure, and her body had sung with delight beneath his skilled fingers. But there was more to the act, and she longed to experience everything. He'd eased her initial fears with fevered kisses and seductive caresses. She now knew two things: she wasn't frigid in the bedroom, and Gareth would never lie to her.

She'd never thought to trust a man again, but Gareth was different. Hadn't he proven himself trustworthy?

Jane summoned her maid, dressed in a rose alpaca morning gown, and rushed down to see if there were any messages on the vestibule table. She had no appetite for breakfast and settled instead for a cup of coffee in the dining room.

She had almost finished her first cup when there was a knock on the front door. She ran to open it, beating her elderly butler to the task.

Gareth stood on the front step.

"Thank goodness it's you!" she cried out.

He arched a dark eyebrow. "I should be so fortunate as to always receive such a warm welcome."

Jane was aware of her butler coming into the vestibule. "Lady Stanwell?"

She waved him away. "No need for concern, Graves. I will see Mr. Ramsey to the parlor myself."

Once they were alone, she shut the door and leaned against it. "Did you find the duke?"

He chuckled at her eagerness. "I did. I sent Lady Olivia

a note reassuring her of her fiancée's well-being before coming here."

Jane let out a sigh of relief. "Olivia must be so relieved."

"Not all went smoothly, Jane."

"What do you mean?" Her eyes snapped to his face, and it was then that she noted his appearance. His clothing was disheveled, and a faint bruising appeared by his right eye. His bottom lip was split at the corner. "What happened to you?"

"The moneylender is not a gentleman, but a man known for his hard tactics. Needless to say, there was a scuffle."

She came close and gently touched the corner of his lip. "You fought to save Edward."

"It was the expedient thing to do at the time. Snake did indeed mistake the duke for his younger brother and decided to send a message that he was late on his loan. The timing of my arrival was most fortunate. You should know that the duke is battered and bruised, but will recover just fine."

Her breath seemed to solidify in her throat. "Oh, Gareth," she said.

"No need to worry now. It all ended well."

She gently touched the bruising under his eye. "This will surely turn black and blue."

He smiled. "I've had worse."

"And your lip! Are you in pain?"

"Not overly so, but I do enjoy your ministrations."

"Devil," she teased. "Is that all you think about?"

"Only when I'm with you."

Her heart lurched. He surprised her yet again. He'd risked his safety to aid her close friend and her fiancée.

Leaning close, she placed a gentle kiss on his bruised lip.

"Jane," he groaned, and pulled her into his arms.

Emboldened, she kissed him again. "I want to finish what we started last night."

He arched a dark eyebrow. "Here? Now?"

She smiled coyly. "No, but soon."

A wicked glimmer lit his eyes. "I'm at your service, madam."

Her heart skipped a beat at his charm.

*Oh, dear.*

She'd sworn never to care for a man again, and heaven help her, never to love again.

But the heart—especially hers—was unpredictable and uncontrollable. It never seemed to listen to reason.

# Chapter Fifteen

After Gareth left, Jane busied herself with the mundane task of taking inventory of the pantry alongside Aunt Eleanor in a vain attempt to keep her thoughts from him. Despite the disorderly shelves full of jarred vegetables and jams, she had only been partly successful. Her mind kept turning to the prior evening and the pleasure she'd experienced.

Gareth had sensed her unease and had seduced her slowly, carefully, until a passionate fluttering arose at the back of her neck and her fear had dissipated. Until her body throbbed with pleasure and she'd eagerly craved more…so much more. Until Olivia had banged on the front door and interrupted them with her crisis.

"My lady?"

Startled, Jane knocked over a jar of jam on the shelf. Her butler stood in the pantry doorway.

"Yes, Graves."

"There's a gentleman caller for you," he said.

Gareth had only departed two hours ago. Jane's brow furrowed. "Has Mr. Ramsey returned?" she asked.

"No. Mr. Marbury waits in the parlor."

An unpleasant feeling rose in her throat. She hadn't seen Simon since she'd abruptly left Vauxhall Gardens with Gareth. Jane turned to explain Simon Marbury's presence to her aunt and a found a wide smile lighting the elderly woman's wrinkled face.

"My, my," Eleanor said. "You have become quite popular with the gentlemen lately. I am proud of you, my dear."

"It's not what you think," Jane rushed.

Eleanor shooed her out of the pantry and to the door. "Go. Meet Mr. Marbury in the parlor. You do not need to explain yourself to me."

Her unconventional aunt was turning out to be even more open-minded when it came to Jane's widowed status. Jane wondered how receptive Eleanor would be if she knew exactly what Simon had planned for her the night of Vauxhall Gardens.

Squaring her shoulders, Jane swept into the parlor. Simon jumped to his feet from the sofa as soon as she entered. He was meticulously dressed as usual with an olive green jacket, flowered waistcoat, skintight pantaloons, and buffed Hessians. She couldn't help but compare his delicate features with Gareth's rugged masculinity and, not for the first time, she wondered what she had found attractive about Simon.

Would he have aided Olivia? Would he have gone off to unsavory parts of London in the middle of the night to brawl a cruel and dangerous moneylender?

The answer was a resounding no.

"Thank you for receiving me. I was concerned for your

welfare after you left Vauxhall Gardens," Simon said.

She recalled Gareth unceremoniously announcing she'd been ill from imbibing too much alcohol. She'd been mortified at the time, but looking back, it was an effective way to allow him to escort her home.

"I do believe I drank one too many glasses of your potent punch," she said. As if he didn't know. As if he hadn't planned on getting her intoxicated.

Simon stepped toward her, hands clasped behind his back, and an expectant expression on his face. "I apologize if I offended you in some way that evening."

She saw no need to mince words. "I was taken aback by what you wanted. Especially regarding Lord Hartley."

"I thought you sought excitement. You seemed to be enjoying our attention that evening," he said.

She straightened. "I did. But I believed any excitement would solely be between the two of us, and certainly not while I was too foxed to know what I was doing."

"And now?"

She shook her head.

"I take it your affections have been occupied elsewhere?" he said.

"Yes."

"I see. Mr. Ramsey is a lucky man." His voice was resigned.

Simon was too intelligent not to know, but still she asked. "Why would you assume I'm involved with Mr. Ramsey?"

He gazed at her with a bland half smile. "Come now, my lady. I saw the way he looked at you. It was merely a matter of time."

She felt a strange thrill at his words. Did Gareth really look at her with avid interest? Enough to make it known to Simon and others? She recalled Lady Preston's blatant interest in Gareth. She'd believed Gareth was caught up in the lady's seductive trap.

Simon shifted uneasily on his feet, and her eyes snapped back to his face. She didn't need to apologize, but something about his distress, no matter how much of it was from his own vanity, prompted her to speak. "I'm sorry, Mr. Marbury."

"Don't be. I hope you find what you seek."

"You as well."

He cleared his throat. "I should like to remain friends. My family is hosting its annual ball in a month. Mother is excited, even though my father remains ill with little chance of recovery. Your friend, Lady Olivia, and her mother are attending. The duke and his grandmother, the Dowager Duchess of Westmont, as well. I hope you will still attend?"

Jane recalled receiving the invitation. The ball was two weeks before Olivia's wedding, and she had previously intended on going.

Simon stared at her intently, waiting for her answer. It suddenly occurred to her that—once again—he was concerned with what society thought. Not of her reputation, but of his. She had been seen with him at the theatre and at Vauxhall Gardens. Society believed she was out of mourning and that Simon had taken an interest in her. He gloried in the attention. Relished it. He would surely be mocked if she didn't attend his family's ball and it became known that the tragic widow of Lord Stanwell had lost interest in one of the *ton's* favorites, the fashionable Mr. Simon Marbury.

Or worse, that she chose another over him.

"I had planned on attending, but I'm uncertain if—"

"Mr. Ramsey is attending as well," he said.

She blinked in surprise. Gareth had not spoken fondly of Simon. She recalled his words and the stiffening of his features as he'd spoken them.

*"We are involved in business matters, but we are not friends,"* Gareth had said.

After what he had told her about Simon's plans for her at Vauxhall, she'd thought Gareth would avoid socializing with Simon. Certainly not attend a silly ball.

Not for the first time, she wondered exactly what business dealings Gareth and Simon did have together. Did Gareth represent Simon in a legal capacity? But how could that be if Gareth solely handled matrimonial matters?

Her curiosity was piqued. What was the connection between the two men? She may go to the ball, but she wanted the truth beforehand.

It was time to put the question to Gareth directly.

# Chapter Sixteen

The Marbury foundry and factory was located on the outskirts of London. It was a cavernous stone building. Carts loaded with charcoal were lined along one side of the factory and a stream flowed parallel to the building and powered a churning water wheel. Thick black smoke curling from the factory's two smoke stacks marred the clear-blue sky. Gareth had purposely arranged his meeting with Simon at the foundry late in the afternoon, after the hottest part of the day had passed.

Simon met him at the tall wood and steel doors at the entrance to the factory. "What happened to your eye?"

Gareth touched his bruised left eye and grinned. "I enjoyed a few matches in the boxing ring with a colleague."

Simon snorted. "It wasn't our mysterious investor, was it?"

Gareth grinned and shook his head. "No such luck. He hasn't changed his mind about remaining anonymous either. But he did insist I tour your factory and report back to him."

Gareth stepped through the doors. The heat level rose

twenty degrees, and combined with the thick smell of burning charcoal and melting iron the air was oppressive. The sounds of the blast furnaces were distinct and loud.

"I come to the factory only when it's required of me. The heat and stench are overwhelming," Simon said, pressing a handkerchief over his nose and mouth.

Both men wore white shirts and dark trousers. Gareth had never seen Simon dressed so simply.

"With your father ill, I assumed you would spend a lot of time here," Gareth said.

Simon snorted. "My father loved the foundry. I prefer my office in the comfort of my own home."

No wonder. With his polished Hessians and styled blond hair, Simon appeared out of place in his own factory. Even his callus-free hands and buffed fingernails, without a hint of dirt beneath them, were a tell-tale sign of his life of leisure.

"Show me where the cannons are manufactured," Gareth said.

They ventured deep into the foundry where two blast furnaces, tall chimney-like structures, were operating. Large, muscular men in dirty shirtsleeves and soot-blackened, weathered faces shoveled charcoal into one of the blast furnaces. The fire roared like an angry dragon as the charcoal burned brightly hot in the belly of the furnace. The temperature was stifling, and beads of sweat ran down the men's foreheads. Another worker tossed ingots, or bars of pig iron, into the top of the furnace.

"Who supplies your iron?" Gareth asked.

"An iron ore mining company North of Manchester. After they mine it, they smelt the iron into ingots. Our factory remolds the pig iron into the cast iron cannons," Simon shouted over the noisy furnaces.

Simon motioned to one of the workers, and a burly man with bushy brows and sweat-soaked shirt approached. "This is Mr. McGiltry, the foundry manager. He'll explain what they're doing."

"We're casting the barrel of the cannon now," McGiltry shouted as he pointed to a worker pouring red-hot liquid iron into a long, cylindrical mold. "Every cannon has a cone with an internal cylindrical bore for holding an explosive charge and ball. The thickest and strongest part of the cone is sealed close and located closest to the explosive charge. That's the next step in our casting. When the explosive charge ignites and the ball leaves the bore, the thickest portion of the cone contains and directs the force."

"Do you manufacture other things?" Gareth asked.

"Aye," McGiltry said. "The foundry also produces cast iron fire grates, balustrades, and parts for steam engines."

"Thank you, Mr. McGiltry," Gareth said.

Simon led Gareth away. "The majority of our production is cannon manufacturing. Before my father fell ill, he signed another contract with the Board of Ordnance to supply cannons to the army."

Gareth had a file on the Marbury Company and already knew this information. Simon's father was a true innovator. He had also been known as an ethical businessman. His illness was a tragedy, not only because old man Marbury wasn't expected to recover, but because his son would inherit everything.

Simon's father had created a lucrative business, but his son had managed to go through the profits by gambling, drinking, and visiting expensive brothels. His clothing and tailor bills were outrageous, not to mention the gross amount he lavished on himself and his friends with private theatre boxes at Drury Lane and private supper boxes at Vauxhall Gardens. He was a spendthrift and derelict.

He was also a criminal.

"I'd like to see the finished product," Gareth said.

A hall connected the foundry to a large warehouse that stored the manufactured cannons. As soon as they left the stifling heat of the foundry, Gareth breathed easier.

He ran his hand down the length of a cannon's black barrel. The cast iron was stamped with the words, "MARBURY COMPANY."

"My investor wants to maximize profits," Gareth said.

"I can do this," Simon said.

Gareth held his gaze. "He wants to know the details."

Simon pressed his lips together, then finally nodded. "It's the pig iron. Too much phosphorous makes the pig iron excessively brittle. Phosphorous cannot be removed during the smelting process. My supplier has phosphorous-free ores, but they are scarce and expensive and found only in a few mines. I'm careful to purchase high quality pig iron. But I've placed orders for the cheaper type as well."

Gareth understood. "You said the inferior pig iron makes the cast iron brittle. Won't the cannons fail?"

Simon's mouth turned upward in a sardonic smile. "I admit they may have a tendency to burst during operation without showing any previous weakness or wear."

"Doesn't it make them dangerous to operate?" Gareth asked.

"Perhaps." Simon shrugged. "Or perhaps not. Either way, the army's contract is fulfilled."

A flash of pure rage went through Gareth's spine at Simon's cutthroat business practices. By sheer force of will, he forced himself to rein in his temper.

"I'm not a fool. I don't use the cheaper iron for every cannon," Simon continued, oblivious to Gareth's rising fury, "but when I do, the profit is astronomical. You can reassure our investor that those profits will continue."

Gareth walked around the room, studying the cannons in the warehouse. He wondered what type of iron was used to manufacture each one. "Are any of these here made of the inferior iron?"

"Only one. See if you can find it."

He was not a metallurgical expert, and the cast iron barrels all appeared identical.

"What about the military inspectors?" Gareth asked. "From what I've been told, there are a dozen army men who inspect the cannons. Won't the inferior iron be detected?"

Simon scoffed. "I've ferreted out those inspectors who can be easily bribed."

Gareth's gaze sharpened. "Which ones?"

Simon's eyes were sharp and assessing. "I've told you before, my list is confidential. All you need to know is that the bribes I pay do not put a dent in my profits. Now, have I shown you enough to satisfy your man?"

Gareth had tried to get Simon to reveal names before, but he'd refused to budge. Gareth was frustrated, but he acknowledged the factory visit wasn't an entire failure. He'd learned how the inferior cannons were manufactured. He was only missing one last piece of key evidence.

Which military inspectors were turning a blind eye to Simon's scam? How far up the chain was the corruption?

Simon preferred his luxurious home office, and without a doubt Gareth knew the missing information would be located there. He needed to search Simon's home. Once he had the names, it would be sufficient to arrest Simon and the corrupt government officials.

He'd conducted clandestine searches of homes in the past. He'd once broken into a judge's chambers during a mission to prove the man had been repeatedly bribed to issue false verdicts. Gareth didn't have qualms about breaking into the Marbury's Mayfair mansion.

Gareth kept his face still, his expression bland. "What I've seen should satisfy our investor."

A glint of satisfaction flashed in Simon's eyes. "Good. I need to purchase more pig iron. I'll need additional funds in a month, the same time of my family's ball. How soon can I expect payment?"

Gareth's lips curled in a smile. He didn't need to sneak into Simon's home, didn't need to go to any extremes to get the list of corrupt inspectors. The perfect opportunity had fallen into his lap.

"This is sufficient for my man. I shall give you the rest of the money the morning after the ball," Gareth said.

A smug smile curled the corner of Simon's lips. "Good."

*Good, indeed.*

# Chapter Seventeen

The following afternoon, Jane instructed the hackney driver to drop her off in front of Gray's Inn. She'd never previously visited one of the four Inns of Court. The only time she'd needed a solicitor was after Charles had died and her husband's will was read. The lawyer had conveniently come to her home.

Jane stepped from the hackney and stared at the building that loomed before her. Gray's Inn resembled a sprawling, quaint country house surrounded by an open field of well-tended lawn and trimmed hedges. She followed the gravel path through a brick Gatehouse and was directed to the second floor where the barristers' chambers were housed.

She found herself in a long torch-lit hallway lined with brass nameplates. Halfway down the hall she spotted a nameplate announcing the chambers of Mr. Gareth Ramsey. Her hand hovered over the door handle, and she experienced an overwhelming curiosity to see Gareth's chambers and learn more about him.

Opening the door, she swept inside.

A small vestibule was lined with rows of file cabinets. The scent of freshly brewed coffee made her mouth water. A thin young man with spectacles sat behind a desk stacked with papers scribbling on a legal looking document. Quill in hand, he glanced up and frowned at her.

"May I help you, Miss?" he asked.

"Lady Stanwell to see Mr. Ramsey, please."

"Do you have an appointment?"

She should have expected him to ask. Still, she hadn't come all this way to be denied. "Yes," she said.

The man's lips quirked, and Jane suspected he knew she was lying. If he was Gareth's clerk, he would certainly know his schedule. For an instant, she feared he would turn her away.

She straightened her spine, clutched her reticule firmly before her, and forced herself to look the man in the eye.

His brown eyes shone with intelligence behind his lenses. "I'll tell him you're here, my lady." Setting down his quill, the clerk stood and grasped a crutch leaning against the desk that she hadn't noticed. She was shocked to realize he only had one leg; the other had been removed from just above his knee.

The clerk made his way down the hall, knocked on a closed door, and disappeared inside.

She heard muffled voices, and moments later, the clerk came out followed by Gareth himself.

He looked strikingly handsome in a linen shirt, cravat, and form fitting trousers. His hair was ruffled as if he had run his fingers through it in agitation. His shirtsleeves were rolled up, revealing a sprinkling of dark hair on his muscled forearms. She'd been right about his eye, and he sported a faint bruise that somehow added to his appeal. Her heart did a little jolt at the sight of him.

"Jane! What a pleasant surprise," he said.

He held his office door open.

"Will you need anything further from me this evening, Mr. Ramsey?" the clerk asked.

"No need, Stevens. Have a good evening," Gareth instructed.

Stevens nodded, repositioned his crutch, and departed down the hall.

Jane admired Gareth for hiring the clerk. Charles would never have hired a crippled servant, even if his duties were solely clerical. Her husband had been vain and insisted the servants possess a certain look and carriage.

Jane entered Gareth's office, and he closed the door behind them and took her cloak.

Her eyes traveled over the spacious room. A large pedestal desk sat before a window. A tall stack of papers beneath polished stone paperweights was neatly piled in the corner of the desk. A blotter, pen, and inkwell were in the opposite corner, and a map of London was pinned to the wall. A dark blue jacket rested across one of the chairs, and looking at his rolled up shirtsleeves, she suspected she'd caught him at the end of his work day.

Two chairs in front of the desk and a striped sofa in the corner offered seating for his clients. A dainty sideboard held a crystal decanter of amber colored alcohol and several glasses. Her eyes were drawn to the gold scales of justice upon the mantle. It was clearly a busy barrister's office, and she was fascinated to see where he spent much of his time.

"I don't know why you've come, but I'm thrilled you're here," he said softly.

She looked at the stack of papers on his desk. "I hope I'm not interrupting."

"Not at all. I don't have any more appointments for the day. I can think of no one else I'd rather see." He motioned to the sofa. "Please sit."

He joined her on the sofa and stretched his long legs before him. Looking into his handsome face, she was suddenly filled with unease about her visit.

At her silence, his brow furrowed. "Is something wrong? Is there trouble with the duke?"

"No, no, nothing's amiss. I can assure you that Lady Olivia is happily nursing the duke as we speak."

"Then why come all the way here?"

Her composure was as fragile as an eggshell. She took a deep breath and gathered her thoughts. "Simon paid me a visit."

His gaze sharpened. "Why?"

Anxiety fluttered in her stomach. "He asked about the upcoming annual ball his family is hosting. It's one of the most popular events of the Season, and Lady Olivia is attending with her mother, the Dowager Duchess, and the Duke." She knew she was babbling.

"And you?"

"I've decided to go. There will be at least a hundred people in attendance. It will be safe and I will be sure not to drink anything Simon offers me."

His eyes had a sheen of purpose. "I will look after you."

"So you are attending as well? I had thought you disliked him. At least the way he treats helpless, intoxicated women."

He scowled at the reminder. "I have limited business dealings with him, and I'm obligated to attend."

The time had come. She needed to know what was going on, that her newfound trust in Gareth was not a mistake.

She struggled to keep her voice light. "Yes, about that. Exactly what business do you two have together?"

He waved a dismissive hand. "It's nothing of consequence."

If he thought she would be easily dissuaded, he would soon learn she was not the type of woman who would back down. "I thought you handled matrimonial matters."

"Not entirely. My legal practice includes other types of cases as well."

She searched his face. "I need to know. Why are you working together?"

"It doesn't concern you," he answered in a tense clipped voice that forbade any questions.

Anger rose to her defense. "If Simon Marbury is as depraved as you led me to believe, then why do business with him?"

He glared at her, and a shaft of fire shot at her before his lashes lowered to veil his eyes.

What was going on here? Instinct told her there was more involved than what he was revealing. She'd learned the hard way not to ignore her gut when she thought something was amiss, and it was important to her to learn the truth. He was acting strangely and it was clear he didn't want her to pry. But if it was a simple legal arrangement, then why was he so secretive?

"My business dealings with him began long ago. Long before he got you drunk at Vauxhall," he said.

If he intended to scare her off, she wouldn't be intimidated. "What is it you're not telling me?"

"If you must know—"

Her chin thrust forward. "I must."

Gareth's jaw tightened a fraction. "The Marbury family is in trade. They manufacture cannons. His father had a stroke and has been ill. Simon's running the factory. I'm helping him with a sale of a part of the business."

She blinked. "That's all?"

"That's all. Nothing more." He reached for her hand and gazed in her eyes. "I would never lie to you, Jane."

A tight knot inside her eased. Looking into the hard planes of his face, she realized she had indeed acted foolishly. She suddenly felt ashamed and guilty for doubting him. He had helped her on more than one occasion and had proven himself worthy of her trust.

"I'm sorry. It's just that Charles lied to me throughout our marriage. I swore never to allow a man to make a fool of me again," she said. She couldn't go through that again, and she didn't know if she'd be able to continue seeing Gareth if he was keeping secrets from her.

"You needn't worry about that with me," he said, his voice firm and soothing at once.

The relief she felt was nearly overwhelming. Impulsively, she threw herself against him. Powerful arms came around her, holding her close, and she nestled against his chest. She was aware of the strength and warmth of his flesh through his fine linen shirt, and her heart pounded an erratic rhythm. Chemistry flared between them, drugging and intoxicating.

She tilted her face to his, and he lowered his head and kissed her. His mouth played with slow sensuality over hers, filling her with pleasure and igniting her desire. She clung to him, ran her hands up his arms, feeling the hairs on his muscular forearms, then higher to clutch his broad shoulders. He deepened the kiss, and she eagerly met his languidly seeking tongue with demand.

Blood coursed through her veins like an awakened river. She wanted more warmth, more heat, and pressed herself closer, molding her soft curves to the hard planes of his chest. It wasn't enough. She wanted to be naked beneath him.

Overpowered by him. Consumed.

His hands cupped her breasts through her gown, and she arched forward for his touch. Her nipples turned diamond hard, and she desperately wanted to remove her gown, to feel his large hands stroke her naked skin. For years she'd been lonely and starved, not understanding what she was missing, until Gareth had come into her life and made her feel wanted, craved…desired.

Her fingers tangled in his hair. "Gareth."

"Hmm."

He kissed the sensitive spot behind her ear, her throat, then trailed his lips to the tops of her breasts above the bodice of her gown. Her eyes slid closed. Her breaths grew ragged, and she turned hot and feverish with need.

"Send a carriage for me tonight," she breathed.

He hovered above her bodice for an instant. "I don't know if I can wait that long," he hissed, then licked her cleavage with a slow, hot stroke of his tongue.

*Sweet Lord!* She didn't either.

Her eyes cracked open and the afternoon light filtered through the window. She was struck by the time of day and where she was. "Are you sure we're alone?" she said.

He lifted his head and a strange look flashed in his eyes. "My clerk has left for the day, but you're right. This is madness. It's just that you're so wonderfully responsive. I lose control. Forget where we are." His deep voice simmered with barely checked passion.

Did it really matter if it was late afternoon and not the night? If his clerk was gone, then they were truly alone…

His moist breath was hot against her nape. "We can't do this here. You're a lady."

She didn't want to be a lady right now. She wanted to be naked beneath him.

He sat back and raised her chin with a finger and lifted her face to his. Stark need blazed in his dark eyes, and titillating shivers raced through her.

"The carriage. Tonight," he said hoarsely.

*Oh, yes.*

• • •

After Gareth hailed a hackney and watched Jane drive away, he headed back into his chambers and poured himself a glass of whiskey. Collapsing on the sofa, he took a long drink.

The faint scent of her lavender perfume remained. Lust consumed him. If he didn't have her soon, he would go mad. She occupied not just his erotic fantasies while he slept, but his waking thoughts as well. Nothing could be more dangerous for him as an agent for the Crown.

She'd only known disloyalty and lies from her husband. Gareth knew he was no better. He'd looked into her eyes and told her that she didn't have to worry about deceit from him.

He was a thousand times worse than Lord Stanwell. He was a well-practiced manipulator by trade. As a barrister, he'd never lied to the courts, but neither did he reveal the full truth. He'd learned the art of omission. Tell only what was required of him. He'd served his clients well.

As a spy, he'd learned to outright lie. To do whatever was expedient to accomplish his goals. Lie, cheat, steal…even kill if necessary.

His current mission was no exception, even more so since it had turned out to be more challenging than he'd initially believed. He'd thought it would be easy to entice Simon Marbury into revealing his hand, but his nemesis was cunning. Gareth knew he could handle the mission. Whether it required him to break into Simon's home or sneak into his office during the upcoming ball, he would do it.

But Jane had complicated matters. He was forced to deceive her, to use her—and yes—to outright lie to her. He could do all these things, but for the first time it bothered him to do them. He lusted after her, but he'd also come to genuinely like her. And for one terrible moment, as he looked into her beautiful eyes, he'd wanted to tell her the truth.

*Hell no.*

Nothing could be more dangerous. He couldn't allow his control to falter. He needed to bed her, to possess her. Only then would this madness end. Their time together was limited. He would complete the mission and never look back. It would be simple. The alternative was unthinkable.

# Chapter Eighteen

Late that night, Jane adjusted the hood of her cloak and stepped out of the elegant carriage. Excitement buzzed in her veins as she walked the path to the rear entrance of Gareth's town home. The moon hung low in the sky like a silver coin, illuminating the flowering bushes and hedges. The fragrant scent of rose bushes filled her senses.

Once again, the door opened before she could knock.

"I've been waiting," Gareth said.

He swept her into his arms, kicked the door shut, and claimed her mouth in a bone-melting kiss. His chest was like a wall of granite, and her flesh prickled with excitement. Unlike her first time here, she felt no nervousness, only an urgent need to experience more of what he had shown her.

More desire. More pleasure.

More of *him*.

She grasped his shoulders, then reached up to spear ten fingers into his hair and kissed him with all the pent up desire inside her.

He groaned and tore his lips from hers. "Careful. Or I'll take you right here, right now, on the kitchen floor."

Her pulse skittered at the raw urgency in his voice. Sweeping her into his arms, he carried her upstairs and to his bed.

His handsome face looked dangerous and wicked in the flickering candlelight. His strength and size, which had once intimidated her, now thrilled her. She reveled in his muscles and powerful shoulders. She longed to unleash his fiercest passion. In the short time since she'd known Gareth, he'd completely changed her outlook on intimacy between a man and a woman. The experience was so different from the listlessness of her passionless marital bed.

This was molten fire in her veins. Sizzling and dangerous.

Yet she had never felt so safe and secure.

So cherished.

She glimpsed the hard planes of his face, and a tingling thrill ran down her spine. She had known all along, hadn't she? She was falling in love with Gareth Ramsey.

He hurried up the stairs with her in his arms. Once again there were no servants in sight, and she was grateful for his consideration. He set her on her feet upon the Brussels carpet in his bedchamber and closed the door. A fire burned low in the grate, and a candelabrum was lit on the mantle. Taking her hand, she thought he would lead her to the large bed, but he stopped before the cheval glass mirror and stood behind her.

He pulled the pins from her hair, and her tresses fell to her shoulders and cascaded down her back. Sweeping her hair aside, he kissed the wildly beating pulse at her nape and whispered, "Don't move."

He unhooked the top of her gown, and the satin bodice gaped. Slipping his hands inside, he cupped her breasts with his large hands, and brushed his thumbs against her nipples, turning them hard. She gasped at what he was doing to her, and liquid heat flooded her limbs and pooled between her thighs. She longed to turn and kiss him, but his big body was pressed against her. She was too shy to see herself in the mirror, and she turned her head aside and closed her eyes.

More hooks followed. He slid the sleeves down her arms and the dress slid down to her feet. With a tug of ribbons, her chemise and drawers followed, and she was naked save for her white stockings and frilly garters.

She burned with her need to kiss him. "Gareth," she breathed.

His mouth trailed a path down her shoulder and back. "You're so beautiful," he murmured. "Look and see." Cupping her chin, he turned her to face the mirror.

Stunned, she looked at herself in the mirror. Her hair cascaded wildly across her shoulders and down her back. Her lips were swollen, her face flushed with arousal, and her nipples pebble hard. Candlelight licked the hollows and curves of her body.

She'd never felt beautiful in the bedroom. But now, looking at herself, with Gareth standing behind her, she felt magnificent…like a seductive goddess.

Her eyes met Gareth's in the mirror, and her heart hammered in her chest. He'd touched her with sweet caresses so far, but the hunger in his eyes revealed much more.

*He looks like he wants to ravish me!*

Like a courtesan trained to please her lover, she turned sinuously and wrapped her arms around him.

He swept her into his arms and carried her to the bed.

He left long enough to impatiently strip off his clothes and toss them on the floor.

His body was all sinew and muscle, and she eyed him with appreciation. A sprinkling of dark hair covered his chest and narrowed to a thin line down the corrugated muscles of his belly, then lower still. She experienced a pang of fear at his thick, long manhood.

As she watched, fascinated, it moved, growing harder.

Heavens! Charles had never…

Then he joined her on the bed and all thought fled as naked flesh touched naked flesh. Her breasts were sensitive as they rubbed against his chest, and set her nerve endings on fire.

His lips grazed her ear. "Do you know what I want to do to you?"

Her breath caught at the raw honesty in his voice. "Tell me."

"First I'm going to kiss your lovely breasts." He lowered his head to lave her breast and tug on her nipple. Her heart leapt, as though he'd flattened his palm against her chest and tugged on her most secret longings.

"And then?" she asked breathlessly.

He smiled slyly. His palm trailed down her body until his fingers splayed across her stomach, his thumb grazing the curls between her thighs. "Then I'm going to lick you here until you shudder and cry out with pleasure."

She inhaled sharply. The image of him touching her with his mouth was shocking and arousing at once. "And then?" her voice was a throaty whisper.

"Then I'm going to make love to you until you come all over me."

Her heart thundered in her chest. His words set off tremors

that heated her thighs and groin in delicious anticipation.

His lips traveled down her body, kissing a fiery trail from her breasts, to her stomach and hip. He nudged her thighs apart, cupped her bottom with large hands, and blew his hot breath on her most secret center. She raised her head in surprise, but at the first stroke of his tongue, her tension and nervousness eased in a rush of pleasure. Every nerve ending in her body fired as he made love to her with his mouth. He laved and licked with wicked skill and when he stroked across her sensitive bud, it was the most sinfully sensual act she'd ever experienced. As her pleasure built, she arched restlessly beneath him. She knew what she was reaching for now, but she wanted more, she *needed* more. She longed to be intimately one with Gareth.

Panting through slightly parted lips, she tugged on his hair until he raised his head. "I want you. Make love to me, Gareth."

He loomed above her, his expression one of pure male satisfaction and lust. "You're magnificent," he said in a hoarse voice.

She twined her arms around his neck and pulled him close. He needed no further encouragement. He positioned the throbbing head of his shaft against her core and slowly circled her wet, aching heat. Her body sang with liquid fire, and she dug her heels into the mattress and raised her hips. He slid an inch inside her.

Her eyes closed as she surrendered completely. This was what she'd craved since their first night together. She arched her hips, wanting to feel all of him. Another delicious inch.

"Oh, yes," she panted.

She wasn't a virgin; there would be no pain. Only pleasure.

He lunged forward and sheathed himself to the hilt. She gasped at the incredible fullness. Nothing had prepared her for his size. For the throbbing, pulsing fullness deep inside her. Her body seemed to melt and stretch to accommodate him.

His breath was hot against her ear. "Ah, Jane. It's heaven to be deep inside you at last."

He began to move within her with maddeningly slow strokes. She loved the hot sliding friction and the weight and warmth of his body on hers was intoxicating.

He looked into her eyes, their connection all-consuming. "I fear I'll never get enough of you."

His words stripped the last vestiges of her defenses, touching a vulnerable part of her that she'd kept locked away. A spurt of hungry desire spiraled through her, and she turned urgent in her need. She scratched his back, dug her fingers into his buttocks, and wrapped her legs high about him.

He grunted and finally unleashed the full force of his desire. He was pure power then, commanding her body with erotic mastery. She reveled in his raw passion, and the thrill of his arousal carried her to greater heights. She sculpted her hands over the sleek rippling muscles of his arms and chest. She matched his strokes, their bodies in exquisite harmony with one another. Their moans melded together, heating the air between them.

She'd been missing the rapture of a skilled lover all these years. Yet she knew it was because of him, because of Gareth, and no other man could make her heart and body come alive like this.

She was poised on a precipice of pleasure, and with one more stroke, she soared over the edge to a shuddering ecstasy.

Burying her face against his throat, she kissed his moist skin. Then Gareth stiffened above her and cried out her name with a groan of completion, his manhood throbbing and thick as he spilled his white-hot seed inside her.

. . .

Gareth rolled to his side, taking Jane with him.

His heart pounded and his breathing was ragged. He'd planned to go slow. Planned to show Jane what she could feel, erase memories of her insipid and cold marriage bed. But she was incredibly responsive in her passion, and she'd stolen his will. His control had snapped.

Christ. It was the best sex he'd ever had.

He kissed the top of her head and pulled her close. "I'm sorry. Did I hurt you?"

She looked up at him, brushed his hair from his brow, and smiled. "No. I want to do it again."

His cock stirred in agreement.

"It was never like that with Charles," she whispered.

It had never been like that for him, either.

She ran her hand down his chest, and desire pumped through Gareth. He should be sated. Wanting to sleep. Certainly not wanting sex this quickly. She'd bewitched him. There was no other explanation.

"Don't think of your husband." He knew he sounded surly, but he disliked the thought of her thinking of another man in his bed, even if she did admit that what they'd shared was exceptional compared to her past.

She smiled sweetly and smoothed the frown lines from between his brows. He felt it again. His chest tightened at the hard pull. The relentless tug of unfamiliar emotion. Emotions he was helpless to fight.

She brushed his lips and arched against him. His cock grew and there was only one place it wanted to be. Deep inside her.

Again.

And again.

He vowed this time he would go slowly, easily, the way he'd planned from the beginning.

She sighed and wrapped her legs high about his back and squeezed. He slid inside her welcoming slick heat. Her thighs were surprisingly strong, her inner walls milked him. His nostrils flared from the pleasure and he met her urgency with deep thrusts. He worried he was riding her too hard, then her hands cupped his buttocks, her nails digging into his flanks, and at the same time she bit his neck. All thought left save for the pleasure.

The night exploded.

# Chapter Nineteen

The following weeks passed quickly for Jane. She received more social invitations each day. Masques, balls, garden parties, teas, wedding breakfasts, and christening invitations were delivered. She accepted a few and declined the rest. Her motives were simple. She wanted to spend more time with Gareth.

When he'd send a note for her to arrive earlier one evening, he'd surprised her at his door. "I want to take you for an evening meal."

"Aren't you worried we'll be seen?"

"No. Dolly's is off Paternoster Row and it's famous for its steaks and turtle soup. It's also not the type of establishment that's frequented by the *ton*. Barristers and solicitors eat there. I've reserved a table in a dim corner."

"How exciting."

After feasting on a delicious dinner, they sat and enjoyed each other's company. Jane sipped her wine and was filled with curiosity about him.

"Tell me something about yourself. What was your childhood like? Your upbringing?" she asked.

"It wasn't very pleasant. My parents had a cold marriage. My father had a title, but no money. My mother had a substantial dowry, but no title. It was a convenient match, but hardly a love one."

"Your father shares Charles's vice of gambling. Did he neglect your mother?" She could hardly lift her voice above a whisper when she asked.

"My mother died ten years ago. But during her life, the baron rarely had time for his wife or his children. He spent most of his waking hours at his clubs and managed to drink and gamble away almost all of her dowry. I have too many memories of screaming matches between them as a child."

She stilled. "I'm sorry. It must have been horrible."

He shrugged. "It was upsetting as a young boy, but I no longer think of it."

She knew that couldn't be true. Childhood years were critical and sculpted one's adulthood. She suspected Gareth's past had made him the man he was today.

"My older brother has it worse. He's the heir and must deal with the baron on a daily basis. He's left waiting to inherit what remains, whereas I took my own path years ago," he said.

"As a barrister," she offered.

He nodded. "The baron didn't approve at first. Now I believe he's grateful I'm not asking for an allowance from the family coffers."

"Do you speak to him at all?" she asked. "Olivia told me there are rumors that you are completely estranged from him."

A faint look of amusement crossed his face. "Do they? The rumors are not entirely true. I speak to the baron on occasion. I visit my brother on holidays. But it's also best if I don't speak with my father about anything other than trivial matters such as the weather. I know I'll never turn him away from the gaming tables or his clubs."

Just like she hadn't been able to stop Charles from going to the track. It was so sad. She longed to reach out and touch his hand across the table, but restrained herself. Tonight was not about dredging up upsetting stories from the past, but to enjoy a leisurely dinner together.

"I understand why you became a barrister, but why handle the types of cases you do?" she asked, changing the topic of conversation to something lighter.

His lips curled in a smile. "You mean why represent disgruntled, married gentlemen?"

"Yes."

"I didn't plan it. I had a strong stroke of luck and obtained a divorce for a viscount, which required an Act of Parliament. After word got out, an endless stream of gentlemen began flooding my chambers. The work chose me more than I chose it."

She didn't want to insult him, but she wanted to know. "Has it tainted you?"

He swirled the wine in his glass. "I suppose so. Each client has their own history, whether it's about cheating spouses, wives who are cold fish in bed, or those that have overbearing and unbearable mothers. Others claim their wives suffer from melancholy or are spendthrifts. The list is endless."

"You must have many stories to tell."

He chuckled. "This morning I met with a client who believes his wife is dallying with the head gardener. He claims she insists on eating asparagus at dinner and has an abundance of gas every night to keep her from his bed."

"Goodness! I wonder what she says about him?"

"He asked me how to be rid of her. I told him to buy the woman flowers and take her to dinner at an establishment where asparagus is not featured on the menu. He may be surprised at the result. Needless to say, he wasn't very pleased with me."

Jane burst out laughing. "I wish I'd witnessed it!"

Gareth reached across the table to clasp her hand. "You have a wonderful laugh. I love hearing it."

Her heart pounded, and she smiled. "I haven't laughed in a long time. I have you to thank for it."

He squeezed her hand. "Thank you for accompanying me tonight. There's no one I'd rather spend time with."

His words wrapped around her like a warm blanket. "I enjoy hearing your stories, and I suspect you are being modest. You must be very good at what you do."

He stilled. "You should know that I haven't always treated women favorably in the courtroom. A trial for criminal conversation is never pleasant. I'm adept at sifting through a client's anger and bitterness to extract the most pertinent and favorable facts—anything I can use in a court of law to paint a sympathetic picture of the husband. I'm not known to be a nice person."

She understood. A wife's adultery was often revealed, rarely the husband's. "It's your job to represent your client."

"Perhaps. But the truth is it had never been difficult for me. Until lately. I find I don't enjoy it as much as I used to. My motivations have changed since my earlier days when I'd been first called to the bar. I fear my clients' incessant displeasure has taken its toll. I'm not proud of some of the things I've done, and I've been thinking of handling different types of cases."

"Then you should. I have faith you'd be a success in any chosen area. I also believe life has a way of shaping us. Sometimes our dark past can turn out to be a shining light. If I hadn't lived through Charles's suicide, I wouldn't have been searching for a lover. I would most likely have remarried and never met you."

"You are a treasure indeed, my lady." His thumb slowly circled her hand, and he placed a hot kiss in the center of her palm, sending delicious shivers marching up her arm. A palpable, sensual tension grew between them, and there was no mistaking the invitation in the smoldering depths of his eyes.

"Gareth," she breathed.

"Shall we leave?" He stood and held her chair.

A quick carriage ride later, they arrived at his home. Breathless with excitement, they rushed upstairs hand in hand. They kissed hungrily as she tugged on his jacket and waistcoat until they were discarded. When her fingers tried to work the buttons on his shirt, he aided her by tearing the fabric and tossing it aside. He cupped her bottom and pressed her to him, letting her feel the extent of his desire for her.

Arching her back, she offered her breasts to him. He kissed her eyelids, her lips, the lush swell of her breasts above her bodice until she was aflame with need. She was impatient to have him, all of him, and she grasped his hand and placed it on her silk stocking beneath her gown. He understood what she needed, thank heaven, and his fingers skimmed her slim leg, past her garter to her bare thigh, until he found the moist heat between her thighs.

Clothing fell to the carpet with tantalizing gasps and low groans until nothing was between them but soft skin against sinewy muscle. He picked her up and she wrapped her legs around him as he slid into her.

"*Ah,* Jane," he groaned, his breath hot against her ear.

She buried her face in his throat as his manhood throbbed and pulsed hard inside her. He didn't bother to carry her to the bed, but began moving as he held her. One stroke, two…and her pleasure peaked in an exquisite climax. His body went rigid, and his rough growl of completion pounded through her heart, head, and soul as she held him tightly to her chest.

• • •

The remaining weeks until the Marburys' ball were a whirlwind for Jane. Olivia's highly anticipated status as a duchess required a considerable new wardrobe, and Jane was happy to assist her friend. Jane's days were spent accompanying Olivia to the dressmaker for fittings, shopping for bonnets and accessories, and visiting the shoemaker for colorful ballroom slippers to match the new stylish gowns.

However busy Jane's days were, she looked forward to her nights filled with rapture in Gareth's arms. She would sneak out past midnight and return before sunrise. Aunt Eleanor had commented that Jane appeared happier than she'd been in a long time, but she'd never suspected the reason.

Jane knew the truth.

She was in love with Gareth. And their nights of passionate lovemaking had awakened her body as well as her heart. She'd never felt so alive.

Or so happy.

Certainly not during her three year marriage. Looking back, she realized what she'd felt for Charles had never been true love, but the infatuation of a young girl. He'd been a handsome and charming man during their engagement. She'd been easily smitten and envied by all the debutantes during her first season on the marriage mart. She'd known he enjoyed horses, but what gentleman of the *ton* didn't gamble? Young and inexperienced, she hadn't realized the truth until well after the wedding.

But she was a woman full grown now and—thanks to Gareth—she understood what it felt like when a man took care to pleasure a woman in the bedroom and not just see to his *own* pleasure.

Finding a skilled lover had been her goal all those weeks ago, although she'd never intended or wanted to fall in love. To the contrary, she'd believed herself weak-natured and feared love like the plague.

But no longer. She understood the risks and was willing to continue their affair. Only this time her eyes were open. Gareth cared for her, she was certain. He may not love her, but neither would he lie to her.

A warm glow flowed through her. It was all wonderful and miraculous; something she'd never believed would happen to her again.

She trusted Gareth Ramsey.

Completely.

# Chapter Twenty

Jane dressed carefully the night of the Marburys' ball. She chose a white satin dress trimmed with silver tissue and wore tiny white rosebuds in her upswept fair hair. In a daring move, she'd ordered the dressmaker to lower her bodice, and her breasts swelled above the embroidered neckline. A diamond necklace glittered at her throat. Glancing in the looking glass, she knew she didn't dress for the *bon ton,* but for Gareth.

"You look lovely," Aunt Eleanor said from the doorway. "You've changed and I'm happy for it. May I assume it's due to a certain man's interest?" Her hands rested on her cane as she looked at Jane with avid interest.

Jane's breath quickened, and her cheeks became warm at her aunt's mention of Gareth. "Yes."

Eleanor walked into the room. "The gentleman that had briefly made an appearance at the door a few weeks back? The same man who you swore had no interest in you whatsoever?"

Eleanor asked, a mischievous twinkle in her eye.

Jane lips curled in a smile. "I have been known to be wrong before."

"I'm glad to hear you say it." Eleanor came close and smoothed Jane's skirts. "The silver tissue is wondrous. You should always wear light colors. I dreaded that horrible black."

So did Jane. "Olivia said the same weeks ago. I do believe I'll have every mourning gown burned."

Eleanor stomped her cane. "Huzzah!"

Jane kissed her aunt's wrinkled cheek. "I do wish you could come."

"My dancing days have long been over. I much prefer the comfort of the sofa in the parlor." Eleanor patted Jane's hand. "I would like you to invite your gentleman for dinner one evening. I desire an official introduction."

Have Gareth over to meet her aunt? Jane didn't think he'd want anything to be that official. "He may not want to—"

"Hush, darling. Don't waste time arguing," Eleanor said, motioning to the door. "You must hurry now. The coach is ready."

• • •

The Marbury home was an imposing mansion in Mayfair. The family was not titled, but the wealth Sir Marbury had accumulated was ostentatiously displayed. The glittering ballroom was elegantly decorated with silk wallpaper, priceless artwork by Gerard TerBorch, Jan Steen, and Joshua Reynolds, and dazzling chandeliers holding hundreds of candles. The room was a whirl of brightly colored silks, polished parquet floors, and dozens of liveried footmen carrying trays of expensive champagne.

Gentlemen smiled as Jane passed. Several openly stared. Others came forward to request dances and scribble on the pasteboard dangling from her wrist. Simon Marbury stood beside his mother across the crowded room, his sleek blond hair gleaming beneath the candlelight from the chandeliers. He waved when he spotted Jane.

The women also smiled at Jane in acknowledgement, yet many eyed her with jealousy behind fluttering fans. The gossip had changed, she realized. The malicious and humorous glances behind fans had been replaced with envious glimpses.

How fickle the *beau monde*.

Jane took a glass of champagne from a servant's tray as she scanned the crowded ballroom. She had eyes for only one man tonight. She spotted Gareth talking to a distinguished group of elderly gentlemen. He looked strikingly handsome in a navy coat of superfine, snowy cravat, and breeches. He met her eyes, then said something to the men and walked over to where she stood.

His gaze was riveted on her face, then moved over her body slowly. His slow sensual smile made her pulse race. "You look enchanting tonight, Jane."

Something intense flared through his entrancement, and she had to fight an overwhelming need to be close to him. To touch him.

He eyed the pasteboard dangling from her wrist. "I've noticed your dance card is filling quickly. I want to carry you away from all these admiring fools."

"Jealous, are you?" she teased.

"Furiously so."

His tone was light, but the predatory, possessive look in his dark eyes was not. A titillating thrill shot through her. Did he care for her more than just as a casual affair?

Dare she hope?

"What if I let you carry me away tonight after the ball?" she whispered.

A devilish look came into his eyes. "I'm tempted not to wait."

A tremor inside her heated her thighs and groin. She wanted him to know how much she desired him, how much he affected her senses. She sipped her champagne and licked a drop of bubbling fluid from her full bottom lip. "I'd rather not wait as well."

His eyes now smoldered with fire. "You'll be the death of me, my lady."

A combustible spark flared between them. The raw desire in his eyes made her stomach flutter. For a startling instant, she feared every guest in the ballroom would see the sparks of sexual attraction between them.

"We must be careful tonight," he said.

She understood his meaning. Gareth was concerned for her reputation and wanted their illicit affair to remain secret. Jane understood and was grateful. It wasn't only her reputation at stake, but that of her beloved aunt. Eleanor might be happy that Jane no longer mourned Charles or suffered from the aftereffects of the suicide, but she would be distressed if a scandal developed and Jane was gossiped about. Discretion was the safest course of action. And if her relationship with Gareth changed and progressed, then a proper courtship would be in order.

There it was again. Thoughts of a future. It wasn't possible. Was it?

"Jane!"

Jane started and turned to see Olivia approach, accompanied by her fiancée, the Duke of Westmont. Dressed in a peach colored gown trimmed with an abundance of flounces and frills, Olivia looked as delicate as a china doll. Her face was currently flushed with happiness.

"We haven't had an opportunity to properly thank Mr. Ramsey," Olivia said.

The duke stopped before Gareth. An average looking man with brown hair and eyes, Edward made up for it with a regal bearing. He currently sported a black eye and bruised cheek. "I do believe I owe you a debt of gratitude."

"It's not necessary, Your Grace," Gareth said.

Gareth's bruises had faded after his scuffle with the moneylender and his henchmen, but Edward's bruises were much more prominent. The young duke looked like he recently stepped out of a boxing ring.

"I may look a fright, but my twin looks worse," Edward said.

Gareth's eyes narrowed. "William went to the moneylender after that night?"

"No. William hasn't the courage. We had fisticuffs afterwards. I won." Edward's voice was filled with satisfaction.

Gareth grinned. "I hope it teaches your brother a lesson."

The duke looked forlorn. "I don't know if William will ever learn. But I've decided not to come to his aid so quickly in the future."

Gareth nodded grimly. "It's not easy to stand by and do nothing. But sometimes a man has to learn on his own."

The duke's mouth twisted wryly, and he raised the glass in his hand. "I'll drink to that, Mr. Ramsey."

. . .

Jane's dance card did indeed fill, and she danced the entire evening with eligible bachelors and distinguished gentlemen alike. Gareth did not ask her to dance, but she was aware of his presence in the ballroom. She knew the gentlemen he spoke with, the time he spent on the terrace, and the women who brazenly glanced at him.

The supper room opened before midnight. Her eyes scanned the room just as they had all evening. No matter how foolish, she longed for Gareth to escort her inside.

Simon appeared at her side instead. "Shall we?" he asked, offering her his arm.

She hesitated. "Are you going to offer me your arrack punch?" she asked, half in jest and half serious.

He had enough sense to look duly admonished. "Come now, I promise to act the perfect gentleman. Don't you believe me?" he said with a grin.

She did. At least for tonight. She smiled at his charm, and placed her gloved hand on his sleeve.

A group of society matrons were watching. Jane recognized them as the same women who had maliciously gossiped about her at Olivia's engagement ball. The same women who'd sent her running to the terrace rather than face her tormenters. It had only been little over a month ago, but it truly felt like years.

She was no longer the same woman—no longer the doomed widow whose husband placed a pistol to his head and took his life. The nightmares had ceased along with her despair. Her affair with Gareth Ramsey might be a secret, but it openly affected her confidence, her bearing…her very essence. She had changed and was no longer a subject of pity.

Simon escorted her toward the supper room. A wicked thrill raced through Jane as the women stared at her with avid interest and jealously.

She knew Simon was using her, but at that moment, she didn't care. Let everyone believe he was with her tonight and would eventually move on to the next woman. For now, she was enjoying every minute of their envy.

An hour later, Jane was seated beside Olivia and the duke when she spotted Gareth across the room walking toward the open French doors. She assumed he was headed for the terrace to smoke a cheroot with fellow gentlemen, but at the last second he turned left and exited the ballroom through a side door.

Curiosity combined with a hint of mischievousness welled within her. Did he seek a private spot to escape the crowd and heat of the ballroom? She'd spent little time with him tonight, and she longed to steal a moment alone with him.

She rose and excused herself under the guise of having need of the ladies' retiring room. Following behind a pair of chattering matrons with tall, jeweled turbans, she slipped through the same door she'd seen Gareth use.

Wall sconces illuminated a black and white marble hall. Spotting no servants or guests, she ventured further. The corridor branched off into numerous hallways that led to different parts of the house. Aubusson carpet runners and portraits of Marbury ancestors decorated the dimly lit halls.

Music from the ballroom faded as she ventured farther from the ballroom.

Looking right and left, she didn't see a single soul and was about to return to the ball just as she spotted Gareth's tall, broad shouldered frame mid-way down a long hall. Opening one of the doors, he slipped inside.

What the devil?

She followed, her footsteps silent on the plush runner. Numerous closed doors lined the hall. She tried to recall which room he had entered. The first room was a vacant conservatory with violins resting on chairs, music stands with sheets of music, and a pianoforte. A few steps further, she pressed her ear to the next door and thought she heard a faint sound.

She cracked it open.

It was a study with a mahogany desk, tall bookshelves lined with books, and a pair of leather hammerhead chairs situated before a fireplace. Gareth's back was to her. He was busy pulling out drawers from the desk and rummaging through them. He was clearly searching for something. One of the drawers was locked, and he withdrew two rods from his waistcoat pocket and started picking the lock.

She froze in stunned tableau.

Seconds later, the lock sprung free and he began searching through the drawer. Withdrawing a piece of foolscap, he slipped it into his jacket pocket.

What was going on here?

She must have made a strangled sound for his head whipped around to spot her in the doorway. She froze, her hand stiff on the door handle.

"What are you doing here?" he demanded.

His voice was cold and flat, unlike any tone she'd heard from him before.

"I—" Instinctively she took a step back. He was by her side in a flash. Grasping her arm, he pulled her into the study and shut the door.

"I thought to have a moment together," she blurted out.

His expression was hard as granite. "You shouldn't have followed me."

Her eyes darted to the open desk drawer. "What on earth are you doing?"

"It's best if you leave. Now."

Her stomach knotted, and she stiffened under his withering glare. She didn't understand. She was not only confused by what she'd witnessed, but by the harshness of his voice. "What's going on here?"

"I haven't much time. Go. Now."

A cold wave entered the room. She had a sickening feeling, similar to one she'd experienced years before. When she'd caught Charles in his first lie. She'd ignored her instincts then.

She refused to ignore them now.

"No," she said firmly. "Not until you tell me what you're up to."

He cursed under his breath and speared his fingers through his hair. Several heartbeats passed, and she thought he wouldn't answer.

"I'm not solely a barrister," he said.

Her mind whirled. His explanation made little sense. "What on earth does that mean?"

"I work for an organization."

"Who?"

He shook his head. "There's no time to explain."

"Who!" Her voice rose an octave.

His eyes lowered, shadowing his expression. "I can't tell you."

She opened her mouth to protest, to insist he tell her what he'd taken from the desk, when he silenced her by pressing a finger to her lips.

Footsteps sounded outside the study door.

A split second later, the door handle turned.

"Damn!" he muttered beneath his breath.

Jerking her into his arms, he tossed her onto the desk, hiked up her skirts, and stepped in between her legs. He closed the desk drawer that he'd lock picked moments ago, and claimed her lips just as the door opened.

"What's going on here?" a familiar masculine voice demanded.

Jane could barely breathe beneath the steely strength of Gareth's body pinning her to the desk. With his lips smothering hers, she couldn't speak. She pressed against the solid wall of his chest to no avail.

Gareth lifted his head and turned to the doorway. Over his shoulder, she glimpsed Simon's surprised face.

"This room is occupied," Gareth drawled.

Jane pressed more insistently against Gareth's chest.

His gaze returned to her, his dark eyes unfathomable. "Please," he whispered so low only she could hear.

She froze, his weight still pinning her down. He was asking her to go along with his ruse.

Questions hammered at her, but she didn't want to insist upon answers in front of Simon. Looking up at Gareth, she nodded slightly, enough for him to understand. Gareth stepped back, and Jane slid ungracefully off the desk. Heat flooded her cheeks as she straightened her skirts.

Simon's gaze met hers. "I knew you were a woman of passion, Lady Stanwell. My only regret is allowing Ramsey to win your affections."

She would perish of embarrassment. "Ah, well…I'm sorry."

"Don't be. I don't mind you two together; however, I must insist you leave this room," Simon said.

Jane was happy to oblige Simon. Head held high, she walked to the door. Gareth was on her heels.

Halfway down the hall, he grasped her gloved hand. "Thank you."

She whirled on him. "This isn't over," she said. "I want the truth."

"I told you—"

"Yes, yes. You're not solely a barrister and you work for a mysterious organization," she snapped. "That's not good enough. I want to know the whole truth."

His fingers tightened on hers. "Shh. Not here."

She refused to be put off. Refused to be lied to.

"When?" she demanded.

"I have to deliver something. Let me escort you home."

*Deliver something?* Her spine stiffened like steel and she raised her chin in defiance. "Does it have to do with what you took from Simon's desk drawer?"

He shot her a murderous look that made her back up a step. She'd never seen him like this. Intimidating. Ruthless. Focused.

Alarm bells rang in her head, her heart. Something was terribly wrong. She'd learned the hard way never to deny her instincts.

Twice was enough to last her a lifetime.

# Chapter Twenty-One

Gareth struggled with what he could tell Jane. He should be angry that she'd followed him and disrupted his search. He should balk at the thought of telling her the truth. But he didn't. And not only because there was no other logical explanation for why he'd been rummaging through Simon Marbury's desk drawers. He wanted to share the truth with her, wanted to share his deepest secrets with her.

And that was not only disconcerting, but impossible.

He was sworn to secrecy. Every mission was vital and no one, other than a spy's contacts at the Home Office, knew the details of an assignment. If an agent broke this vow, he put everyone at risk.

Gareth grasped Jane's arm and steered her down the hall. "Come with me and I'll explain. My driver will take you home."

Her step faltered and she looked up at him in the dimly lit hall. Her delicate brows knit, and he knew a war waged within her. She wanted to believe in him, but she was afraid.

At last she nodded, and relief flooded through him with an intensity that was startling. There it was again. The foreign tug in the center of his chest. The uncomfortable feeling he was too close, too keenly aware of her feelings, her needs, and wanting to make everything right for her. She was making him *feel*, dammit.

Once in the vestibule, Gareth waved to one of the Marbury's footmen. "The lady is unwell. Please have my carriage brought around," he instructed.

His carriage arrived, and Gareth helped Jane inside and took the seat across from her. She looked beautiful bathed in the light from the carriage lantern. Her flaxen hair and tawny eyes beckoned to him even more than the tempting swell of her breasts above the provocative bodice of her gown.

As soon as the carriage jerked forward, she whirled upon him. "What do you mean you work for an organization?"

He was almost relieved at her anger. He'd rather face a furious Jane than a tearful and distraught Jane. "I cannot reveal the details."

"You said you'd explain everything," she said.

"I'm doing the best I can."

Anger flared in her eyes, and her face flushed.

"I'm sorry, Jane. I am sworn to secrecy."

"I thought you were a barrister," she accused.

"I am."

"I thought you were aiding Simon with the sale of a portion of his family's business?"

"That isn't exactly true. All I can say is that there's unsettled business between us."

"Then why sneak out of the ball to search Simon's study? Why not simply ask him for what you need?"

His fingers fisted. He hated talking about Simon with her. It was difficult enough watching the blackguard escort Jane into the supper room. He'd wanted to sprint across the ballroom and slam his fist in Marbury's face. He was unaccustomed to these jealous feelings and he didn't like them. He'd stayed away from Jane tonight to protect her reputation, not soil it with his jealousy.

She was addling his brains. Making him weak and vulnerable at a time when he needed all his wits.

His voice hardened along with his resolve. "Simon Marbury is no good. It's not just his sexual proclivities; he has no qualms about illegal activities," he ground out.

"If what you say is true, then why on earth would you do business with him?" she demanded.

"It was a necessity, dammit." A sudden thin chill hung on the edge of his words.

She flinched at the tone of his voice, but instead of being cowed, her eyes flashed in her heart-shaped face and her spine stiffened. He should be used to Jane's stubborn determination by now. Her chest rose and fell in agitated breaths, and all he could think about was the alabaster smoothness of her exposed skin.

"How long have you known all this about Simon?"

"Since Lady Olivia's engagement ball."

She paled, and he immediately regretted his words. The ball was the first time he'd found her list and learned that Jane actively sought a lover. The first time he'd learned of her interest in Simon.

He should have lied, at the least answered vaguely, but

once again she'd distracted him. Just sitting next to her in the carriage set his nerve endings on fire. She was too intelligent not to piece things together and catch his mistake. Too late, he knew what she was thinking before she spoke.

"You *used* me. All this time, you used me." Her accusing voice stabbed the air.

He attempted ignorance. "What are you talking about?"

"You needed a reason to engage Simon, didn't you? I must have been a very convenient means of doing so. You pried me for information about Simon's whereabouts and you showed up everywhere. Our ride in Hyde Park, the theatre...even Vauxhall Gardens." Her lips thinned with anger.

"I didn't want to. I tried to talk you into removing his name from your foolish list, remember?"

Her beautiful brown eyes blazing, she faced him furiously. "You wanted me to replace him with you!"

"You should have listened."

She glowered at him across the seat.

He reached out to touch her shoulder. Her skin was soft and inviting. "Jane, I never lied about wanting you."

She recoiled. "Don't touch me! Everything about you is a lie. You used me to cover up your clandestine search of Simon's study tonight."

"I wouldn't have needed to if you hadn't interrupted," he pointed out. "I would have been long gone before Simon arrived."

"Fine! Blame me. I could have helped you if I knew what you were about."

"I already told you that I'm not at liberty to reveal the truth," he said tensely.

"What else are you not at liberty to reveal? What's real about you, Gareth Ramsey. Was our affair calculated as well?"

He caught the flash of pain in her face and experienced an unfamiliar ache in his chest. "It wasn't like that."

The carriage slowed to a stop and go pace. From the driver's shouts, Gareth knew they were stuck in traffic. Jane shifted toward the door and reached for the door handle.

"What are you doing?" he growled.

"Leaving."

"Don't be stupid. We're two blocks from your home."

He grasped her by the waist and pulled her onto his lap. He realized his mistake when her lush derriere cushioned his thighs. Lust shot through him with the force of a shot. His heart thundered.

"Don't you dare!" Her voice was laced with panic, not anger, and he knew she felt the heat leap between them. The more she struggled in his lap the more his manhood throbbed.

"Make no mistake, Jane. This is real between us."

She pushed against him. "Don't touch me," she hissed. "I'd be better off with Simon. At least with him, I'd know *exactly* what he'd want from me."

Possessiveness raged with animal instinct. He wanted to push her down on the carriage bench, lift her skirts, and thrust into her body. To mark her. Brand her as his.

The carriage came to a stop before her home. He released her, and she scrambled off his lap.

"Don't do anything foolish," he said.

Her skewering look was like a punch to his gut. "I already have."

Not waiting for the footman, Jane opened the carriage

door and left him.

. . .

This couldn't be happening to her. Not again.

Jane's stomach clenched as she entered the town house. As was customary when she stayed out late, Graves had left a low burning lamp on the vestibule table, and she made her way up the stairs to her bedchamber. Not bothering to wake her maid, Jane collapsed on her bed in her beautiful gown. She was exhausted. The despair she had been holding in check crashed down upon her like an ocean wave. Tears welled within her eyes and slid down her cheeks.

She was a fool. She'd fallen in love with Gareth Ramsey only to learn he was not what he'd seemed.

Charles had done the same thing. He'd covered up his gambling habits for the first year of their marriage. She knew he liked his clubs and the race track, but she believed he enjoyed the camaraderie of his peers. Her father, the earl, had spent hours at White's and Brooke's. Mother had always told her men needed their clubs to be happy.

But then Charles had started spending more and more time away from home. She'd spent hours waiting up for him until she'd been exhausted and had fallen asleep in the parlor chairs. He'd grown distant and agitated. She hadn't suspected money problems until six months later when she was at the dressmakers. The modiste had pursed her lips and mentioned an outstanding bill. Shocked, Jane had gone home to find Charles in the study huddled over a household ledger. He'd been angry when she mentioned the dressmaker and forbidden her to go to the modiste's shop. She'd quickly switched dressmakers.

He'd denied money problems. She'd believed him at first because she desperately wanted to believe.

*Stupid Jane.*

Was what had happened tonight any different? Gareth had lied to her. His story of a secret organization and underhanded business practices with Simon made no sense. Her days of naivety were over. Only this time, it hurt much, much worse. Her heart ached even more than it had after Charles's suicide.

Because she loved Gareth. Truly loved him.

Only to be betrayed by him.

And that was the bitterest emotion of all.

• • •

The exclusive gambling hall in Pall Mall was known for its wealthy clientele and attractive female croupiers. One could count on high stakes play and elegant suppers from a renowned French chef. It was also known for its aged whiskey, fine cigars, and private gambling and billiard rooms.

The proprietor spotted Gareth as soon as he entered the establishment. A few words were spoken, and Gareth left the main floor and headed down a hallway toward the back of the building where the private rooms were located. Not bothering to knock, Gareth opened the last door.

Daniel Forster stood by a snooker table, racking ivory balls on the green felt. He didn't bother to turn to the door when Gareth entered.

"You're late," Daniel said.

"You'll forget it when you see what I have." Gareth pulled a paper from his coat pocket and handed it to Daniel.

Daniel's brow rose as he scanned the contents. "This is exactly what we've been looking for."

Gareth selected a cue stick from a wall rack. "I recognize many of the names. White, Bowen, Fitzwilliam."

"They're all prominent members of the army." Daniel walked around the table, the light from the brace of candles reflecting off his ruby signet ring. "Many were highly decorated after Waterloo. All of them are currently employed as military inspectors of weapons and cannons."

Gareth studied the ivory balls. "Money has a tendency to corrupt even the most honorable."

Daniel's gaze sharpened. "You retrieved this from Simon Marbury's home?"

"I did."

For an instant, Gareth pictured Jane standing in the doorway of Simon's study. Golden curls framed her lovely face, confusion furrowed her brow, and her breasts rose and fell in agitation. Even though he had insisted she immediately leave, her stubborn nature had prevailed. He'd acted as swiftly as he could when Simon had interrupted by tossing her onto the desk and kissing her. Thankfully, Simon had believed the ruse of a passionate encounter. But if he hadn't, Gareth would never have forgiven himself if she had been harmed.

Daniel was watching him closely. If his friend sensed a fraction of Gareth's inner turmoil, he didn't mention it.

Daniel set the paper on the corner of the snooker table. "Excellent work. You discerned how the inferior cannons are manufactured with the cheaper phosphorous infused iron. You identified the corrupt military inspectors."

Gareth took a shot with his cue stick, and the crack of ivory balls rent the air. Three landed in side pockets. "What's next?"

"The Home Office will look into the inspectors. Then we can finally deal with Marbury."

"When can we arrest Simon?"

"We can't. The Crown doesn't want an arrest or a public trial."

Gareth looked up sharply. "What the hell do you mean?"

"The King knighted the father and declared him a hero. An arrest and trial would be a disaster," Daniel confessed. "The newspapers will print all the unsavory details and the scandal will demoralize the army. There's even a fear that citizens may riot."

Gareth glowered at Daniel. "Simon Marbury has to be punished." He'd be damned if he'd allow Simon to escape unscathed. The Crown owed every soldier who was unfairly wounded by Simon's defective cannons justice.

"Simon Marbury will be given a choice: exile to the Continent or imprisonment."

"It's not much of a choice, is it? I suspect he'll leave straightway," Gareth drawled.

Daniel nodded curtly. "I don't like it either. After meeting Private Stevens, I want Simon drawn and quartered." He leaned against the snooker table. "How has Stevens turned out for you?"

Gareth thought of the wounded private. "He's intelligent and conscientious. I've gained an invaluable legal clerk."

Daniel let out a breath. "At least something good has come of it."

Gareth took another shot, this time managing to pocket two more balls. "What will become of old man Marbury? The company?"

Daniel shrugged. "Sir Marbury is in ill heath. There's no sense questioning him or even informing him of his son's illegal activities. As for the company, it will most likely be liquidated by the Crown after his death."

"Good. At least Simon won't be able to touch the money. But I want the satisfaction of informing him of his fate," Gareth said.

Daniel grinned. "I wouldn't have it any other way. You deserve the honor."

"You should know there was a slight complication during my search for the list," Gareth said. Obligation required he tell Daniel all the unforeseen compilations during a mission.

"Such as?"

"Lady Stanwell walked in as I was rummaging through Marbury's study. Thereafter, Simon found both of us together."

"You're kidding? Does Lady Stanwell know you took the list?" Daniel asked.

"She knows I took *something*. We distracted Simon as to my true intent."

Daniel's mouth curled mockingly. "I can only imagine how you accomplished that feat. Did you tell the lady about your mission?"

Annoyance pierced Gareth's spine. "Of course not. I told her I work for an organization. That's all."

Gareth could feel Daniel's sharp eyes boring into him across the snooker table. "You're torn about it."

A muscle ticked at Gareth's jaw, and he set down the stick. "I didn't tell her, dammit."

"You care for the lady. Don't bother to deny it."

Gareth knew Daniel had a right to ask and a right to be concerned, but nonetheless his temper flared. "What if I do?"

"Can you ensure her silence until we gather a case against the military inspectors and Simon Marbury is forced out of the country?" Daniel said.

"Yes."

Gareth hoped so. He needed to see Jane. And not just to ensure her silence. He didn't like the way things were left between them. He didn't like the hurt expression on her face just before she fled his carriage.

"Good," Daniel said.

Beneath Daniel's keen gaze, Gareth had the distinct impression his friend knew not all was good or fine.

Daniel crossed to a desk and placed the list in a drawer. "The list is evidence, but the mission isn't over. Until then you will have to continue to mislead her."

Gareth nodded tersely. What was the matter with him? It shouldn't pose a problem. It should be easy. He'd done it countless times before.

But he'd never cared about another before either. None had silky blond hair and big brown eyes. Nor had they driven him crazy with the scent of lavender soap, lush, kissable lips, and fantastic breasts.

Daniel stepped close and clasped Gareth's shoulder. "Remain steadfast, Gareth. We're very close."

# Chapter Twenty-Two

"I've misjudged a man. Again." Jane said.

Olivia halted and turned to Jane. "What are you talking about?"

They were walking down Bond Street after spending two hours at the dressmakers for Olivia's final fittings. Olivia's maid and footman trailed behind, carrying hat and shoe boxes and numerous packages from their shopping excursion. Jane had been unusually quiet at the dressmakers, and she finally had a chance to talk to Olivia when her servants were far enough away not to overhear.

"Gareth is not who he seems," Jane said.

Olivia eyed her curiously. "Of course he is. He's the son of Baron Suffolk and a barrister. He's a man who's wildly attracted to you."

Jane blinked, feeling utterly miserable. "Those facts may be true, but it's not who he truly is."

"You're speaking in riddles."

"Keep walking." Jane took Olivia's arm and prodded her onward down the street. "I don't wish to draw unwanted attention."

"You're being ridiculous," Olivia said, but she continued strolling arm in arm with Jane.

Anguish seared Jane's heart. "I don't know the entire truth myself. All I can say is I've made a grave error by once again falling in love with the wrong man."

Jane decided not to discuss the details of what had occurred in Simon's library with Olivia. She still didn't understand everything that had occurred herself, but some innate sense told her to keep the knowledge secret. Which was ridiculous, really. Had Gareth trusted her enough to tell her the truth?

Olivia stopped in the middle of the street, and pulled Jane into a nearby shop. The shop's bells chimed as the door closed behind them. Jane was too stunned to protest as the pungent aroma of oolong and green tea filled the space. She found herself by a table stacked with colorful tins of loose leaf tea. The proprietor of the teashop was behind the counter assisting another customer. Olivia smiled, waved, and feigned interest in a tin.

"You're in love with Mr. Ramsey?" Olivia said softly.

A flash of loneliness stabbed at Jane. "I tried so hard not to fall in love, but it seems I'm weak natured," she said in a broken whisper. She picked up a random tin of tea, only to notice it was a medicinal blend for melancholy.

*Perfect,* she mused.

Olivia's sympathetic look made Jane's spirits sink even lower. "Oh, Jane. You're not weak natured, you're a wonderful, loving person."

"I'm a fool," Jane said bitterly.

"What you need is to continue shopping. Nothing helps a lady deal with her difficulties more than a new bonnet," Olivia said, her face lighting as if she had found the solution to Jane's problems.

Jane couldn't help but smile. Everything had always been so simple for Olivia. "No more shopping for me today. I'm quite exhausted."

Olivia frowned. "There are circles under your eyes."

"I've been fatigued of late," Jane admitted.

"Have the nightmares returned?"

"Thankfully, no." She hadn't suffered from the gory images of Charles's suicide since she'd been intimate with Gareth. Looking back, she'd rarely thought of Charles at all over the past several weeks.

"Are you coming down with an illness?" Olivia pressed her hand on Jane's forehead like a concerned mother.

"No. It's simply from lack of sleep," Jane reassured her.

"Over Mr. Ramsey?"

"I suppose."

She didn't want to admit she'd cried herself to sleep most nights since her estrangement from Gareth. She never felt this fatigued when she'd sneaked out of her house and spent her nights in his bed. To the contrary, she'd never felt more alive than in Gareth's arms.

*Don't think of it!*

"Will you give him a second chance?" Olivia asked.

Jane lowered her eyes, feeling utterly miserable. "To what end?" Olivia bit her lip, and guilt pierced Jane's breast. "I'm so sorry, Olivia. Your wedding is next week and I'm burdening you with my problems."

A sudden blush like a shadow spread across Olivia's fair

cheeks. "Ah, Jane…about the wedding—"

Jane's gaze snapped to her friend. "Don't tell me Edward has had second thoughts?" she said sharply.

"No! Nothing like that," Olivia protested.

"Then what?"

Olivia hesitated for a heartbeat. "Edward has chosen Mr. Ramsey to be his witness for the wedding."

Jane flinched. "Please tell me you're jesting."

Olivia swallowed with difficulty and shook her head.

"I see." Jane's heart thumped madly, and she struggled to keep her tone light.

Olivia had already selected Jane to be a witness, and as such, she would be forced to be in Gareth's presence at the ceremony and wedding breakfast. She hadn't seen him since she'd fled his carriage the night of the Marbury ball.

Could she do it? Was she strong enough to be so close to him and not long for his touch? For his kiss?

Olivia gave an anxious little cough. "I'm sorry, Jane. Edward is grateful to Mr. Ramsey for saving his life that night. And his occupation as a barrister makes an excellent choice as a witness. I had no idea you had second thoughts about him. I thought you'd be pleased."

She would have been thrilled. But that was before. A part of her wanted to back out of the wedding and stay hidden in the seclusion of her home. But she couldn't—wouldn't—do that to her closest friend. She refused to act selfishly. Olivia wanted her to stand beside her as she married the duke she loved, and Jane would do it. Even if it meant being in close vicinity to Gareth. She'd just have to do her duty for Olivia and avoid Gareth at all costs.

Jane forced a smile as she squeezed Olivia's hand.

"Please don't worry. Your wedding day will be perfect. It's not as if Mr. Ramsey and I are getting married."

• • •

Jane left Olivia with her servants on Bond Street and hailed a hackney to take her home. She hadn't faked her fatigue, and she was relieved when the conveyance came to a stop in front of her town home. Parting the curtains to glimpse outside, her heart skipped a beat.

Good heavens! Gareth's carriage was waiting by the corner. She easily recognized the black conveyance and matching chestnut bays. It was the same carriage that had waited for her in the back alley and whisked her to Gareth's home each night. Even though it had only been days since she'd eagerly gone to him under cover of darkness, it seemed so long ago.

Maybe Gareth wouldn't see her. Maybe he had knocked on her front door and had been told she wasn't home and he would depart.

Seconds later, she watched in dismay as Gareth stepped out of the carriage and headed for her hackney. A restless energy consumed his long strides.

Her breath caught. The traitorous part of her longed to see him.

No, she couldn't be weak. She had to think with her head and not her heart.

The cab door opened and he was there, hand outstretched to assist her, his unfathomable eyes capturing hers. Her heart started to flutter wildly in her breast. He wore no hat and his windblown jet hair fell across his brow, the silky black strands curling around his ears, softening the chiseled angles of his cheek and jaw. She longed to reach out and stroke his face, trace the pad of her thumb across his enticing lower lip.

"Jane," he said simply.

She had every right to reject him, to push his hand away and step out of the hackney, march into her home, and slam the door in his face. But she was a lady, she reminded herself, and she would act with dignity.

She placed her hand in his and stepped down.

She felt the heat of his hand through her glove. He was so tall, she had to crane her head to look up at him. "Why are you here, Mr. Ramsey?"

He frowned at her formal address. "I wish to speak with you."

"Unless you came to confess everything, there's nothing left to say." Her tone was cold and proper.

Perfect.

"Please Jane, can you forget that night? I miss you. I miss us." Oh, no. She felt her body weaken. Felt the familiar lick of heat between her thighs and tighten her breasts. She forced herself to stand straight, not to sway toward him.

"There is no us." Her voice sounded weak to her own ears.

"May I come inside?"

She shook her head. "No. It's not a good idea."

He had no intention of explaining himself. He wanted her to forget, to look past what had occurred. She'd ignored her instincts with Charles. She would never do so again.

"Very well. I want to tell you that the duke asked me to stand as his witness for the wedding," Gareth said.

She already knew. Thank goodness Olivia had told her.

Otherwise, she would have been highly dismayed at the news. "How prestigious for you."

"Will that upset you?"

She raised her chin a notch. "Why should it?"

"All you need to do is ask, and I shall tell the duke I'm unable to stand as his witness," Gareth said.

Dare she do it? It would be so easy. But another part of her refused to give him the satisfaction of knowing just how deeply his lies had scarred her. She didn't want to regress to the depressive state she'd been in over Charles's suicide and betrayal. She feared the black shroud that had enveloped her for so long would return.

Just then, the front door opened and Graves stood there. She was vaguely aware that they were drawing attention on the busy street.

"Let me come inside," he said.

"No. I'm expecting company."

He looked at her skeptically, and she knew he realized she was lying. "Very well. Another time, then?"

She barely made it into the house and up the stairs to her bedroom. Shutting the door, she slid down its length to the floor as the tears started.

# Chapter Twenty-Three

Gareth stepped inside the Seven Sins brothel in Soho. The scent of cheap perfume, the sight of red velvet drapes and plush settees, and the sound of coarse feminine laughter assailed his senses.

A middle-aged woman with dyed red hair, a heavily painted face, and huge breasts openly displayed in a low bodice approached. Her shrewd gaze raked him from head to toe, and Gareth suspected she was very adept at calculating a man's worth on sight. He recognized her as one of the owners of the brothel from the last time he'd been here with Simon Marbury.

"Looking for some lively sport tonight, my lord? I have a wide selection of women who would be happy to cater to your every desire," she said in a sultry voice.

No doubt. The reputation of the brothel was infamous. The women were ill-treated, often beaten, and nothing was off limits.

"Not tonight. I understand Simon Marbury is here."

She pouted painted lips. "I'm not at liberty to reveal our clientele, my lord."

"Marbury's phaeton is parked round the corner. I assure you, he'll want to see me," Gareth said, a cold edge to his voice.

Her eyes narrowed a fraction as she realized Gareth wasn't leaving until he got what he wanted. "Follow me. Should you see someone along the way you'd like, you have just to say the word."

Gareth followed past a hall with scarlet-painted walls lined with closed doors. Noises sounded from behind the doors—moans, a trill of high-pitched laughter, even masculine sobbing. Women walked past him, all Cyprians who were scantily clad. They eyed him like he was fresh meat and some reached out to stroke his arm. A few were slower to meet his gaze, and they had an unmistakable look of desperation in their eyes. Daniel wanted to find a way to shut down the brothel, and Gareth couldn't agree more.

At last the red-haired woman halted by a closed door. "I'll leave you to your business." She gave him a sly glance. "But you are welcome to share the woman inside if that's what you prefer."

Gareth waited until she left. He banged on the door once, then threw it open.

Simon was on the bed with a young brunette. She gasped and sat up as the door hit the opposite wall. She struggled to cover her naked breasts.

"What the hell!" Simon said.

Gareth glanced at the girl. "You should go."

She scrambled from the bed and grasped her dress. Not bothering to put it on, she fled from the room.

Simon stood and reached for his breeches. "What's the meaning of this?"

"I never liked you, Simon."

"What?"

"Only scum frequent the Seven Sins."

"That's what you came to tell me?" Simon reached for his shirt.

Gareth shut the door and leaned against it. "Not really. I want you to know that I'm an agent for the Home Office."

Simon stilled mid-way through buttoning his shirt. "You've been spying on me? You bastard!"

"I can say the same of you."

"What of your secret investor?" Simon asked.

"He doesn't exist. But the Home Office knows about your faulty cannons and the inferior pig iron you've been using to produce them. Our soldiers have suffered a dire price because of your greed." Gareth glared at Simon as he thought of Private Stevens and his amputated leg. He pushed away from the door and stalked forward. "We also know about the military inspectors you've been bribing to pass the inferior cannons."

Simon's face paled a shade. "I never told you their names."

"You can't possibly think I'm that inept at my job, can you?"

Simon pointed a shaky finger at Gareth. "The night of my family's ball. I caught you in the library with Lady Stanwell. You stole the list of names of inspectors from my desk, didn't you?"

"Rest assured, your scheme is at an end," Gareth said.

"Does Jane know what you were doing there that night?"

Gareth's stiffened. "She has nothing to do with this."

"You bedded her and forced her into becoming your accomplice, didn't you?"

Gareth clenched his jaw. A picture of Jane outside her home crystallized in his mind. He wanted desperately to see her, to hold her. If only she hadn't caught him in Simon's library that night.

"Don't ever speak ill of her," Gareth said tersely. "You're guilty of treason. Now you're going to pay the price."

Simon bellowed in outrage and charged forward. Gareth was ready. He sidestepped and his fist struck Simon in the eye.

Simon hollered in pain and swung madly in a wild attempt to strike his opponent. Gareth instinctively shifted to the balls of his feet, raised his fists, and delivered a swift uppercut, punching Simon square in the nose. Blood spurted across Simon's shirt-front, and he crumpled to the floor.

"You can't do this!" Simon cried out, clutching his bloody nose. "My father was friends with Wellington and was knighted by the Crown. I'm the heir to the Marbury fortune."

"No longer. Upon your father's death, all the company assets will be seized by the Crown. If it was up to me you'd be imprisoned, but the Crown wants you exiled. You have to leave and never return."

"With what money?"

"That's your problem. You have two days to get out of England."

# Chapter Twenty-Four

The wedding of the Duke of Westmont and Lady Olivia, the daughter of Earl Newbury, took place early Sunday morning. It was a warm summer morning as family and close friends occupied the pews of St. George's church.

The Dowager Duchess had complained that the younger son of Baron Suffolk had no standing to serve as a witness for her grandson. The duke never bothered to explain to the dowager that Gareth had saved his life and inadvertently the life of his younger twin, William. The stern-faced woman would probably suffer apoplexy if she knew the truth.

Jane stood beside Olivia and held her bouquet of white roses during the ceremony. She tried desperately not to notice Gareth, but it was impossible for her eyes not to stray to where he stood beside the groom. Gareth's height alone made him stand out, and he was very handsome in a brown coat embroidered with silver and gold, a white silk waistcoat, and brown breeches. He was watching her, his look so intense it was almost like a caress against her skin. She finally gave in to the temptation and turned. Their gazes caught, and her breath hitched.

It was a mistake. So much could be conveyed in one sizzling glance. Her pulse leapt, and she quickly faced the altar.

It took all her effort to stand straight and paste a smile on her face for the remainder of the ceremony. She was exhausted by the time the couple was pronounced man and wife. Her feet hurt. Her back hurt. Even her breasts felt tight in the bodice of her silk gown. She was convinced she was coming down with a cold.

At last the duke and his new duchess strode down the aisle. The guests rose to depart the church in anticipation of the wedding breakfast, which was to take place at the Westmont's mansion.

Jane searched for Olivia among the throng of well-wishers. She started when someone touched her sleeve.

"Jane." Gareth looked down at her, a frown marring his brow. "I couldn't help but notice you look pale. Are you well?"

No. She'd never be well again. She also felt slightly perturbed by his less than flattering observation. "I'm fine."

"I came to see you," he said.

The brush of his fingers on her sleeve upset her balance. He stood so close she could feel the heat from his body. "I know."

"Several times."

"I was told." She'd watched him through her bedroom curtains each time he approached the front door. She'd left explicit instructions for her butler and household staff to turn him away. She knew she was reverting to her former ways of rarely venturing from the town house.

But this was different. She didn't fear gossip about the suicide. That part of her life was behind her. She feared something else entirely.

She feared her own sanity. The days were long, but the nights were endless. He'd shown her the pleasures of the flesh, and she'd foolishly fallen in love.

She loved him still.

His beautiful brown eyes darkened, reflecting flecks of green and gold from the church's stained glass windows. "Please. I don't want to leave things like this between us."

She tried desperately to ignore the all too familiar shiver of awareness in her limbs. She swallowed hard and searched for some kind of armor to wrap around herself. "Leave me be, Mr. Ramsey."

"I may not be able to answer all your questions, but you must trust me."

She'd done that before, and she'd found him sneaking in Simon Marbury's study, picking a desk lock, and stealing documents. She wanted desperately to put her faith in him now. What was it about Gareth Ramsey that made her want to trust him when every warning was that she shouldn't?

She looked up at him then. His dark hair fell in a wave across his forehead, his handsome features focused intently upon her.

It was too much. He was too much. His overwhelming masculinity was overpowering. She longed for the protectiveness of his arms. She wanted to rest her aching head against his broad shoulder, to press her weary body against his.

No. She was weak. She always had been. She needed to

get away. To breathe and think clearly.

"Trust you?" She laughed bitterly, and the dowager turned at her shrill tone.

"I know I don't deserve it—"

"No. You don't." She turned to leave.

"Jane—"

She glanced back, purposely not meeting his gaze. "As I said, please leave me be, Mr. Ramsey. Today is about the bride and groom, and Olivia needs me."

• • •

The following morning, Jane had never felt worse. Although she went to bed early, she woke feeling tired. Throwing back the covers, she sat on the edge of the bed just as a knock sounded on the door.

"Come in." Even her voice was hoarse.

Aunt Eleanor entered followed by a young maid carrying a breakfast tray. The smell of fried eggs and bacon made Jane's stomach roil. She made it to the chamber pot just in time to vomit.

Eleanor shooed the maid away and held Jane's hair as her stomach cramped again and again. A long minute passed as Jane groaned and emptied what remained of her stomach into the chamber pot. After the nausea subsided, Eleanor helped Jane bathe her face in rosewater and held out a towel.

"You're breeding," Eleanor announced.

Jane dropped the towel and looked at her aunt in shock. "It's impossible."

She had never confessed her affair with Gareth to her aunt. She didn't want to shock the woman. And besides, what Eleanor said could not be true.

"I may be old, but I'm not a simpleton. I know you've been sneaking out of the house at night. It's your mystery gentleman, isn't it?" Eleanor said.

Jane's cheeks heated. There was no sense denying it. "I admit to sharing his bed, but what you are implying is not possible. The doctor said—"

Eleanor stomped her cane. "Posh! Those charlatans don't know anything about a woman's body."

"But I was married to Charles for three years!"

"Has it occurred to you the problem was with Charles, not you?" Eleanor said.

Jane was stunned. Could it be true? Could she be carrying a baby?

All her life she'd wanted a child, but she'd believed it impossible. Not only had her marriage been doomed, but her hopes of conception taken after the doctor told her she was barren.

But the telltale signs were present. The fatigue. The nausea. The fullness and sensitivity of her breasts. Thinking back, she had missed her menses. Had her long-ago prayers finally been answered? Could she be carrying a baby? A baby that she could lavish with all the love in her heart. A precious gift.

A child.

*Gareth's child.*

Jane looked at her aunt. "You must tell no one."

"What will you do?"

"Retire to the country. Raise my child. Live happily ever after," Jane said.

Eleanor tsked. "What of the father? The man must do the right thing. It's still early on in the pregnancy. No one will suspect the babe was conceived before the wedding."

"No! There will be no wedding. He's not what he led me to believe."

Eleanor leaned on her cane. "Darling, no one is. The question is: is he a good man?"

*Yes. No.* "I don't know. This is all so shocking. Please, let me think."

. . .

A week later, Jane knew she was pregnant. She woke up violently ill every morning and the nausea would last until mid-afternoon. She wanted to confess her secret to Olivia, but she had departed with the duke to visit his country estate in Kent and wouldn't return for days. Only Aunt Eleanor was aware, and instinctively Jane understood the fewer people who knew about the baby the better.

Jane dressed in a simple morning gown and headed for the small herb garden behind the town house. She picked mint and chamomile, the two herbs that helped with her morning sickness. She breathed in the fresh air, thick with the scent of flowering shrubs and garden herbs, and thought clearly of her future.

She had sworn never to remarry. She had more freedom as a widow than she could have imagined as Charles's wife. She could come and go as she pleased, and thanks to her widow's portion and Aunt Eleanor's generosity, she never had to worry about money.

Only one thing could have changed her mind. Did she want her child to be born a bastard? The thought made her blood run cold. She knew firsthand how cruel society could be. Even if she fled to the country, word would get out that the widow of the Earl of Stanwell had a baby out of wedlock.

What type of future could she offer her child then?

From the beginning, Gareth's mindset had been clear. He never wanted to marry. He didn't want children. He'd wanted an illicit liaison—just as she did. If she told him about the baby, would he feel honor bound to marry? Would he look upon her and their child with regret and dislike for forcing his hand?

He disposed of unwanted wives, for goodness sakes. He'd certainly never wanted one for himself.

Things were even worse now that she'd learned Gareth kept secrets—dark secrets that hinted of dangerous and underhanded activities. She may not know for whom he worked, but she had enough sense to know that it did not bode well to illegally search someone's home and steal documents. Whatever he was involved in, it was clearly unsafe and could put her and her baby in danger. She couldn't allow it.

Her course of action was clear. If she wanted to keep her child safe and she didn't want the baby born illegitimate, she'd have to find another man.

This time a husband and father.

Could she do it? Could she purposely set out to deceive a man into believing the child was his? Could she marry another when her heart was engaged elsewhere?

*Yes.* She'd do anything to protect her unborn baby. Sacrificing herself was a small price to pay.

• • •

Once her plan was set, Jane was able to think things through clearly. Her mood was still heavy, but her spirits lifted slightly when she dressed in a new emerald gown trimmed with Brussels lace. She had originally ordered it from the modiste with Gareth in mind. She pictured him admiring her in the silk and enthusiastically removing it afterwards.

She pushed the erotic images aside. That part of her life was over. She didn't need another man's lies or deception. Taking one last look in the cheval glass, Jane smoothed her skirts and departed from her bedroom.

The dress was meant to flatter and draw masculine interest, and she would use it for that purpose at Almack's tonight. The Wednesday night assembly would be a special night, and not just because Jane intended to flirt and dance all evening, but because Aunt Eleanor felt well enough to accompanying her.

Eleanor waited at the bottom of the stairs. Dressed in a dark blue gown with an embroidered overskirt, her blue eyes twinkled. "Shall we?" Eleanor said.

"I'm pleasantly surprised you feel well enough to attend," Jane said.

"Staying inside is not good for anyone's disposition. I also admit my good friend from my school days, Lady Turner, is visiting from the country with her nephew, and I'm eager to see her. She was always quite entertaining."

Jane helped her aunt as they stepped inside Almack's assembly rooms. She instantly felt the heat. The smell of expensive French perfume did little to disguise the odor of perspiring bodies in the crowded space. The all too familiar queasiness roiled in her stomach.

*Oh, no. Not here.*

"Smile, my dear. The gentlemen are watching you,"

Eleanor said.

Jane obediently smiled as her gaze wandered longingly to the open French doors leading onto the terrace. "Would you like a glass of lemonade?"

"That would do nicely," Eleanor said.

Jane hurried to the refreshment table, which was near the French doors. A cool breeze of fresh air brushed her heated cheeks and lifted the hair on her nape. She breathed in slowly until her stomach settled and she was no longer in danger of embarrassing herself from getting sick.

Sipping a glass of cool lemonade, she scanned the room. She knew Gareth wouldn't attend Almack's. He stayed far away from the marriage mart. Although a part of her longed to see him, she knew it was for the best. She needed to put him out of her mind.

*The baby,* she thought. *Think of the baby.*

She looked about the room with renewed interest. Fetching a second glass of lemonade, she returned to her aunt's side only to find her engaged in conversation with another woman. The lady was close to Eleanor's age and was dressed in a purple gown and tall turban with a matching dyed ostrich feather. She gestured with her hands as she spoke, and the feather bobbed vigorously with her movements.

Eleanor waved Jane over and made the introductions. "Jane, this is my old school friend, Lady Turner." Eleanor turned to the woman. "My niece, Lady Stanwell."

Jane smiled and tried not to stare at Lady Turner's towering turban. She understood why her aunt had called Lady Turner entertaining during their school days. Just then they were approached by a gentleman Jane didn't recognize.

Lady Turner beamed and rested a jeweled hand on

the gentleman's sleeve. "This is my nephew, Captain Liam Turner. Captain Turner, may I introduce Lady Hollister and her niece, Lady Stanwell."

Captain Turner bowed and Jane curtsied. A handsome older gentleman with brown hair and blue eyes, he was dressed in his regimentals.

"May I have the pleasure of this dance?" Captain Turner asked her.

For a brief instant, Jane wanted to refuse. The Captain wasn't Gareth. But that was the point, wasn't it?

She smiled and placed her hand in his. "I'd be delighted."

# Chapter Twenty-Five

Gareth walked into Gentleman Jackson's at 13 Bond Street wanting to fight. He entered the main salon, and his eyes immediately homed in on the large roped-off square ring, anchored with stakes driven into the floor at each corner. He was restless and frustrated, and angry at himself for the cause.

Daniel waited by the ring as an assistant finished tying his boxing gloves. "You're early."

Gareth scowled. "And you're obsessed with time."

The assistant approached to help Gareth with his own gloves.

As soon as Gareth was ready, Daniel dismissed the assistant and came close. "Simon Marbury is preparing to leave the country," Daniel said.

"I know. At least he'll leave with a black eye and a broken nose."

Daniel grinned. "You did well."

"I still think the bastard got off too easy." Gareth also knew what society thought. That the elegant and wealthy Simon Marbury, the *ton's* favorite, had become bored and sought adventure on the Continent. The news had irked him.

"I agree," Daniel said. "He should have been forced to fire one of his own inferior cannons."

"Now that would have been justice," Gareth scoffed. "No more talk. Let's fight."

Both men stepped into the ring. They circled each other, each slightly crouched at the knees, head and shoulders pressed forward. They jabbed and punched as they made their way around the ring, their athletic moves like a well-practiced dance. Their guttural groans and the scraping of their shoes on the hardwood floor echoed off the bare walls as they fought.

Gareth was taller, more heavily muscled, but Daniel was sinewy and quick on his feet. Both got in several solid punches. When Daniel struck Gareth's jaw with a fierce uppercut, Gareth's head snapped back. For a brief instant, he relished the pain as it pounded through his skull.

He narrowed his eyes, focusing on his opponent. In his mind he saw his next move; he'd attack quickly, jab at Daniel's weaker left side with ruthless efficiency. But the pain and something else—something foreign and against every instinct of self-preservation he possessed—slowed his movements.

Daniel took advantage of Gareth's hesitation to land a quick two-punch combination to his midsection. Startled, Gareth staggered backward and doubled over. His ribs ached as he gasped for air. Pain reverberated through his head, jabbed at his stomach, and sparked thoughts in his brain.

He was going crazy without Jane in his bed. Without her laughter, her seductive touch, and God help him, without her company.

Work held no interest for him. No matter how many new cases Gareth took on or how many hearings and trials he conducted at the Old Bailey, his thoughts kept returning to Jane.

Worse still, other women held no interest for him. They all paled in comparison to Jane. He had lust, but only for her.

His attempts to see her had failed. Her elderly butler was like a military sergeant when it came to protecting his mistress. Gareth knew she was home, and he'd spotted her bedroom curtains flutter open as he approached her Piccadilly residence. If this continued, he'd end up forcing his way inside.

His mouth twisted wryly at the thought. Brutality outside the boxing ring wouldn't help his cause with Jane at all.

"Enough," Daniel said, stepping from the ring. His assistant came forth to remove his gloves, and Daniel wiped the sweat from his brow with a towel. "What's the matter with you?"

It took a few more breaths before Gareth was able to answer. "Nothing." He reluctantly left the ring and had his own gloves removed. He wiped his mouth with the back of his hand and saw a streak of blood.

Daniel dipped a dented metal cup into a bucket of water, took a drink, then handed the cup to Gareth. "It's not like you to let anyone beat you to a bloody pulp."

He deserved a beating. His conscience, which had never bothered him in the past, had taken over. He didn't like it.

"You're like a caged tiger ready to pounce, but for some insane reason you're holding yourself back. I'm wary of you," Daniel said.

Gareth took a long drink.

Daniel leaned against the rope. "You needn't be so uptight. The mission was a success. Simon's leaving. The corrupt military inspectors are being dealt with as we speak."

"Good. I need another mission. Tell me you have one in mind." He needed to immerse himself in work. Maybe then he'd be able to think of something…anything other than Jane.

"There will be no future missions for you until you exorcise the demons that are haunting you. You're dangerous and not fit for duty."

"Christ! Is that what you think?"

"That's what I know."

Gareth's eyes narrowed. "Sod off."

Daniel shrugged. "The mission is almost over."

"So?"

Daniel shuffled his feet. "Tell her, man."

Gareth's gaze snapped to Daniel's. "What did you say?"

"You wouldn't be the only agent to confess his secrets to a woman," Daniel admitted.

Gareth knew Daniel referred to their friend Robert and his wife Sophia.

"Are you saying I can tell Jane the truth? The *entire* truth?"

Daniel exhaled as if relieving a great weight upon his shoulders. "I'm speaking as your friend now and not in an official capacity. Use your discretion. I trust your judgment."

• • •

Gareth left Gentleman Jackson's and had taken two steps when he collided into a passerby. He spun about to see a young woman in black and white servant's garb. A hatbox she had been carrying thumped to the ground and rolled to the curb.

"My box," the young woman cried out.

Gareth immediately ran after the package. Retrieving it, he saw that the side of the hatbox was caked in mud. "I apologize, miss. I didn't see you."

It was odd since he rarely collided with anyone, and he wondered how he hadn't seen the young maid. It was almost as if she had intentionally walked into him.

"Never mind that, Monique," a female voice said as an elderly woman with a cane stepped forward.

Gareth faced the woman. She looked vaguely familiar, but he had just taken a beating in the ring and many older women were similar in appearance to him.

"Pardon, my lady. It seems I accidently collided with her." He wanted to say the girl ran into him, but he didn't want the young servant to be disciplined. Her elder employer was obviously wealthy with her fine pelisse and gown, and Gareth knew the rich could be cruel to their servants who depended on them for their livelihood.

"A little mud on a box is no harm, sir. I'm Lady Hollister. And who are you?"

Gareth bowed. "Mr. Gareth Ramsey."

She tapped a gloved finger on her chin. "Ah yes, Mr. Ramsey. I've heard that name before."

No doubt she'd heard of his professional accomplishments. He had no desire to defend himself when the old lady recalled just where she'd heard his name before. He was praised at the gentlemen's clubs, but never in the ladies' drawing rooms over tea.

Lady Hollister suddenly stomped her cane. "I remember now! My niece has mentioned you."

Her niece? Just splendid. He wondered if her husband was his client. "How nice. If you will please excuse me, I must be on my way."

The lady stretched out her cane, blocking his path. "Lady Stanwell. Do you recall meeting my niece?"

Gareth froze. An image of an old woman with a cap the shape of a large mushroom rushing into the vestibule the night he had escorted Jane to her home from Vauxhall Gardens rose to his mind. He'd thought the woman was Jane's housekeeper. Never had he suspected she was Jane's aunt. Lady Hollister may be elderly, but her eyes were sharp and alert, and he had the distinct impression she knew more than she let on.

"I've had the pleasure of your niece's acquaintance. How is she faring?" Gareth asked.

"Ah, one can never quite tell with Jane. A darling girl, she is."

Darling didn't do her justice. Jane was a fantasy in the bedroom.

His fantasy.

"You are a strapping young man. Do you mind helping me to my carriage? My old bones are suffering from shopping for too long," the woman said.

"Of course." He couldn't help but wonder if Jane was waiting in the carriage for her aunt.

Lady Hollister chatted the entire way. Her carriage was parked down the street. She seemed to be managing just fine. He carried the muddied hatbox and her maid trailed behind.

Jane. He wanted to see Jane. His blood ran hot just thinking she may be close.

"Is Lady Stanwell in the carriage?" he asked, attempting to keep his tone light.

"Goodness, no. She's busy with the captain."

"The captain?"

She looked at him as if he was a simpleton. "Captain Liam Turner, of course. The man fancies her. My niece never wanted to remarry, but the captain is so dashing in his regimentals that even she is taken with him. Everyone knows he's seeking a wife."

The hatbox slipped from Gareth's grasp to whack on the ground. His insides twisted.

"Be careful with that, Mr. Ramsey," she chided. "It took me a quite a bit of time at the milliners to find just the hat I was looking for."

"I'm sorry."

Lady Hollister waved a hand. "The hat is for tonight. My niece and I are attending the Vogleson's ball. I'm certain Captain Turner will attend as well." They reached the carriage. "Here we are." Her footman jumped down and took the hatbox from Gareth. "It was a pleasure meeting you, Mr. Ramsey. I assume I will see you at the Vogleson's ball, then?"

Their eyes caught and held. For a brief moment, he couldn't help but wonder whether she had sought him out for just this purpose. He mentally shook himself. It made little sense. Lady Hollister didn't know him, and if she did know the truth between him and Jane, he doubted the lady would want him anywhere near her niece.

He bowed deeply. "I wouldn't miss it, my lady."

• • •

Jane had returned from a walk in the park and was startled to find Captain Turner waiting for her in the sitting room.

Captain Turner rose from a chair as soon as she entered. "Good afternoon." He was well-groomed with cropped brown hair, his crisp uniform, and polished boots. He exhibited an air of command that she'd come to associate with a military man of his rank.

"What a pleasant surprise." She wasn't expecting him. A week after dancing with him at Almack's, the captain had called upon her twice—once with a bouquet of flowers and the second time with a box of chocolates.

He took her hand and led her to the sofa and sat beside her. "I wanted to see you again, Jane."

The thought occurred to her that she hadn't given him permission to call her by her Christian name. Her brows knit. She should be happy by his visit and his use of her name. Surely it meant he was serious in his pursuit.

That's what she wanted, wasn't it?

Her temples started to throb. She feared a headache would be quick in coming. She resisted the urge to rub her temples.

"I find myself most fortunate to have been introduced to you at the first ball upon my return to town."

"I feel the same, Captain Turner."

"Please call me Liam." He squeezed her hand. "It's no secret I've returned to London during the season in the hopes of finding a wife."

She didn't know quite how to respond. A part of her was happy, wasn't it? She needed this. Needed the security and safety he offered for her unborn child. And she required things to move along quickly.

If only she didn't think of Gareth, and compare the captain's established looks to Gareth's virility. Her headache increased in intensity.

"I'm a military man. I prefer things to run smoothly and as efficiently as possible."

Smoothly and Efficiently? He made her sound like one of the soldiers under his command. She inwardly cringed. Would there be no romance as his wife? Would she be expected to obey his commands? Just like one of his soldiers?

It didn't matter. He offered her and her unborn child a safe haven. If she had to rise at five in the morning and perform calisthenics and march in a straight line, she would do it.

He knelt before her and took her hand. "Will you do me the honor of becoming my wife?"

Jane felt the blood drain from her face. She should have expected his proposal. Knew it was coming. Then why did she want to sprint from the room?

If he was disturbed by her hesitation, it did not reflect in his eyes. "I don't have much patience for the reading of the bans and would like to get a special license from the bishop."

She should be thrilled. A special license suited her purpose just fine.

"We must speak with my aunt." Her voice was strained.

His brow furrowed. "You are no longer a minor who needs consent, but a widow of advanced years."

Now he made her sound like an old hag. "I understand. But I would love my aunt's blessing nonetheless."

He nodded curtly and rose. "I shall speak with her straight-way."

His unspoken meaning was clear: it was the efficient

thing to do.

She couldn't help but think of Gareth. His ruthlessly handsome face haunted her. Efficiency was the last word she'd use to ever describe their relationship. If only the smoldering passion she'd experienced in his arms wasn't accompanied with secrets, lies, and danger.

# Chapter Twenty-Six

Gareth circled the Vogleson's ballroom. He felt caged in the crowd of elegantly dressed people. His cravat cut off his air supply, his waistcoat prevented his lungs from expanding, and his coat was too warm. His expression must have been fierce, for several men parted to make way for him.

Gareth scanned the colorful gowns of the women. Where the hell was Jane?

His emotions vacillated between fury and remorse. He kept reliving the moment when his relationship with Jane had gone wrong. A part of him rationalized that Jane didn't need to know why he had been in Simon's study, damn it. It was none of her business. Then his thoughts would turn and he'd want to plead for her forgiveness, her understanding.

She'd turned him into a confused simpleton.

The orchestra changed its tune. Several women were asked to dance, and a small sliver of space opened in the crowded ballroom. At last he saw her.

She nearly took his breath away.

Dressed in a pale rose gown that hugged every delicious curve, Jane looked radiant, even more beautiful than he'd recalled. Her fair skin glowed, her sleek blond hair was upswept, and a fat curl brushed her long nape. Her lush breasts appeared even larger, or had she lowered the bodice of her gown? He felt his skin tighten and his breath caught in his throat.

He was slow to realize she was talking to another man. A military officer dressed in regimentals. She smiled up at him, a slow sexy smile that made Gareth's insides run cold.

He must be the captain Jane's aunt had told him about. Captain Turner wanted a wife and by the way Jane was flirting with him, it looked like she was his choice.

*Never! She belongs with me.*

The captain led Jane onto the dance floor for a country dance. Gareth watched from afar as they came together and parted. Each time their gloved hands briefly touched, he wanted to sprint onto the floor and snatch Jane away from the decorated captain.

At last the dance ended. The orchestra began the waltz. Gareth was on the dance floor in a flash and tapped Captain Turner on the shoulder.

"Pardon, but the lady promised me this dance."

Jane opened her mouth to protest, but Gareth swung her into his arms and into the music.

Even stiff and outraged, she felt wonderful in his arms. He was aware of the harsh uneven rhythm of her breath, of the fire in her beautiful eyes, and of her anger at being whisked away. Silk skirts brushed his legs, and her lavender scent filled his nostrils.

"What are you doing?" she hissed softly.

His gaze was riveted on her upturned face. "I want to ask you the same question."

"Captain Turner is a very admirable gentleman."

He splayed his fingers, the tips just barely brushing her breasts. "Rumor has it he's looking for a wife."

The slight parting of her lips told him she was aware of his touch. But rather than respond, her stubborn little chin jutted forward. "In this instance, the rumors are true. I've decided to encourage the captain's pursuit."

"The hell you have," he growled.

Rational thought fled and he whirled her toward the open French doors and right onto the terrace. "You're not encouraging any man's pursuit, let alone thoughts of marriage."

She gasped. "How dare you! I won't let you speak to me that way."

He held her hand firmly and whisked her down the terrace stairs and into the garden. She had the sense not to scream and draw unwanted attention, but she struggled, pulling against his grasp.

"Let me go," she demanded.

"No."

They passed a fountain, marble statues of Roman gods and goddesses, and stone benches.

"This is outrageous! You have no hold over me."

Drawing her behind the shadow of a large oak tree, he pressed her against the bark. "Oh? What's this?" Jerking her into his arms, he swooped down to capture her mouth.

He knew the kiss lacked finesse. He was nearly ravaging her in his urgency. In the back of his mind, he wanted to slow down, wanted to savor her in his arms and show her how much he missed her. But her stubbornness, her feisty determination, pushed him over the edge and made him dominate her with his strength and the force of his will.

She had to come to her senses, dammit.

Then she melted against him with a sigh, and pleasure coursed through him. Her fingers rose to his shoulders to bury in his hair. His hands explored the soft lines of her back, her waist, her hips. She flicked her tongue across his lower lip with a slow, sensuous lick, and he felt the pleasure all the way to his groin. He experienced a complete thrill of satisfaction.

She knew she was wrong. She knew they were meant to be together.

She parted her lips fully, inviting him to deepen the kiss. He was eager to oblige, covering her lips with his and pressing against her curves. She wiggled closer, rubbing her hips against his, and making mewling sounds that threatened to snap the remnants of his control. She tasted him again, sucking on his bottom lip like a ripe cherry. Raw, sizzling sensation pumped through his bloodstream.

Then she slid her teeth along his lip and bit him.

• • •

"Christ!" Gareth said, rearing back.

Jane jerked out of his grasp and faced him with hands on her hips. "You deserve it for manhandling me in such a fashion."

She stared at his beautiful bloodied lower lip. She'd panicked when he'd whisked her out of the ballroom and kissed her. She feared her weakness would overcome her resolve. And it almost had. She didn't have to fake her response to him. A spurt of hungry desire had coursed through her as soon as he'd pressed her against the oak tree and kissed her. It had taken everything for her to resist him.

She'd actually *bit* him!

She watched half in fascination and half in dread as he removed a handkerchief from his coat and blotted his lip. A small smear of dark crimson marred the white cotton.

"I only wanted you to come to your senses. We have something special," Gareth said.

"Lust is nothing. Captain Turner can give me what I need."

His jaw tightened and his dark eyes looked fierce. "And what is that? He's old enough to be your father. Or is that what you prefer?"

She refused to let him bait her. "Captain Turner gives me honesty."

"You want the truth?"

"I thought I made that clear weeks ago." Her voice was bitter.

"I can tell you now."

She doubted him. He'd concoct lies, just as Charles repeatedly had. It was in their nature. She'd thought Gareth was different, but she had been so easily fooled. "I no longer care."

"Dammit, Jane! I work for the Crown as an agent."

She stilled. She'd expected a story, but nothing so elaborate. "You mean as a spy?"

He nodded tersely. "The Home Office, more specifically."

"Goodness!" Looking into his eyes, she realized he was serious. His admission had her reeling. "How long have you been a spy?"

"Seven years."

"*Seven years!*" she cried out incredulously.

"My assignments have not been continuous. I do have a successful legal practice."

"Why on earth is a barrister working as a spy?"

"I was recruited by a friend. My position at Gray's Inn has come in useful for certain assignments."

Her mind whirled with what he was saying. "What does all this have to do with Simon Marbury?"

"Simon's company has been manufacturing dangerously inferior cannons. British soldiers have been injured."

Her fingers twisted in her skirts. "Is it because of Simon's father?"

"No. Simon purchased cheaper low-grade pig iron for the manufacturing process in order to maximize his profits. The cannons can't withstand the heat and impact of combustion. They fail and injure our soldiers. You remember my law clerk, Stevens?"

An image of the young, crippled clerk at Gareth's Gray's Inn chambers came to mind. "Yes."

"He was a victim of one of Simon Marbury's defective cannons. The bore exploded from the force of the blast and shards of hot iron embedded in his leg. The limb couldn't be saved and had to be amputated. He has a young wife who was pregnant at the time of the accident."

She felt faint. "How horrible." Her voice was barely above a whisper. "You hired him?"

"I did."

Few men would have done so. Charles would not have.

A thought occurred to her. "Is that what you were doing that night in Simon's study?"

He exhaled slowly then nodded. "I was searching for incriminating documents. I found them just before you walked in."

Doubts still remained. Years of disappointment made it hard for her to trust. If everything Gareth said were true, why hadn't she read about the scandal in the newspapers or heard any gossip?

"What will happen to Simon?" she asked.

Gareth's jaw tightened. "He was given a choice to leave the country rather than face imprisonment."

"I heard he was leaving to tour the Continent," she whispered.

"Personally, I believe he should have been arrested and tried at the Old Bailey."

Her eyes snapped back to him. "Why are you telling me this now?"

"The case is over. The bad cannons will be removed from the army's artillery. Simon will be exiled."

"You should have told me. Did you honestly think I'd betray you to Simon?"

"No, it wasn't that. Agents are prohibited from sharing any knowledge of their missions to others."

"Why confess now?"

He clutched her shoulders and gently shook her. "I couldn't stand the thought of you not believing in me, not trusting me."

A ray of hope blossomed in her chest. His confession proved he was an admirable man. Her heart may have been right after all. She thought of the baby, their baby.

She could tell him *her* secret.

"Oh, Gareth," she breathed.

"You must understand, Jane. My work is very dangerous. I've always accepted the risks involved with each mission knowing I was doing it for King and Country."

There was so much more to him. She'd thought him a liar when he was admirable. He'd saved an indigent boy in the park; he'd employed a seriously wounded soldier; and his work as a spy for the government resulted in stopping shipments of perilous cannons to battlefields where English soldiers would be injured by them.

Perhaps there was a chance for them and for their unborn baby. Her heart felt light. The burden she'd been carrying could be shared.

She took a deep breath. "Gareth, I'm—"

He pressed a finger to her lips. "Shh, love. Let me finish. I've so much to say. I've never married for a reason, Jane. My duty is to King and Country. I never know when I'll be assigned the next mission or how treacherous it will be."

Her heart faltered. What was he saying?

"Don't you see?" he said. "Neither of us wishes to marry. I dare not father children or put a family at risk. We were perfect together. We *are* perfect together."

"You like it then? Being a spy?" she asked helplessly.

"I cannot imagine not working for the Home Office."

Her hopes crashed around her. She felt sick. Gareth didn't want to marry. He didn't want children. If she told him she was pregnant, he would act honorably, but he would surely grow to resent her and the child. He liked being a spy, he thrived on the danger.

She wanted so badly to tell him, but the words stuck in her throat. Could she be that selfish? Could she put her child at risk?

She thought of the Captain. He wanted to marry— wanted to obtain a special license from the bishop. It could be done quickly; no one would suspect the child wasn't his.

"I miss you, Jane. I miss our nights together."

Sweet Lord, so did she.

"I'll send my carriage tonight. Come to me."

She wanted to. Oh, she did. But it was no longer simply about her desires. She had to protect her baby.

He caressed her arm. "It can be just as before between us."

But it couldn't be. Nothing could be just as it had been. She was afraid to speak; afraid she'd blurt out the truth in a moment of weakness and then burst into tears.

"No," she managed to say.

His eyes were fierce. "Why?"

"It's too late."

His fingers tightened a fraction on her arm. "Give me a good reason."

She shifted to the side and looked in the direction of the terrace. The ballroom lights flickered, and a trill of laughter floated on the garden breeze. "Captain Turner waits for me."

He dropped his hand from her and stepped back. "You're choosing him?"

She felt the loss of his heat, and a huge, painful knot formed inside her. "It's done."

His eyes grew fierce. "You'll regret it. You'll never experience what we have together with another."

"Good-bye, Gareth."

And for the second time, she walked away from him.

# Chapter Twenty-Seven

The wind howled and rain pounded the roof of the Bear and Bull tavern. The foul weather matched Gareth's mood. He shifted on the wooden bench in the corner and took a good swallow of whiskey from his glass. Despite the fine quality of the alcohol, it tasted bitter.

He never thought it was possible.

He'd grown attached to a woman and developed *feelings*. He wouldn't call it love; he was too cynical to believe in the emotion. He hadn't witnessed it during his childhood with his parents or through his clients in his profession. But he grudgingly admitted he'd developed strong feelings for Jane.

Just like his friend Robert had when he'd first met Sophia.

Only he was more of a fool. He'd been convinced that once he possessed Jane's body, the tightly coiled need inside him would ease. But instead, it was keener than before, driving him to madness. He didn't want their affair to end, but wanted her in his bed once again, desperate to impress the memory of their shared passion in her mind forever. He'd grown fiercely attached to her, and she didn't want him. She'd chosen Captain Turner instead.

He wanted to kill the man.

A tavern maid wandered over. She was pretty, with large breasts the size of melons and red pouty lips. She'd been serving him all night, and from the coy glances she'd given him, he knew what she offered.

She rested a curvy hip on the table, inches from where his hand held his empty glass. "If you've finished with your whiskey, my shift is over," she said.

"Is it now?" His gaze roved her face and rested on her big breasts. A peep of nipple was visible above her frilly bodice. She must have tugged the fabric down before she returned to his table. He sure as hell would have noticed that nipple before.

She leaned close and whispered. "You'll need to rent a room upstairs."

It would be easy to get lost in willing female flesh. The problem was he didn't want her. He didn't want any other woman but Jane.

*Christ.*

"I'll have another whiskey."

The tavern maid pushed away from his table with a pouty expression. "It's only alcohol ye'll be wantin' tonight, then?"

He nodded curtly. "Sorry to say so, but yes."

A knowing look crossed her face, and she shrugged a bared shoulder. "She must be worth it," she said, then wandered off to fetch him another whiskey.

Loud voices in the corner of the tavern caught his

attention. Two men argued. One stood and pushed back his chair. It looked as if there would be fisticuffs tonight. Gareth shifted in his seat. He was itching for a fight, and the big man looked like he could pack a solid punch. If the boxing ring wouldn't satisfy the raw ache inside him, perhaps a good bar fight would.

The tavern owner rushed over, spoke harshly to them, and one of the men stormed out.

Damn.

The door swung open again, this time with a blast of cold wind and rain. A tall man walked inside. His greatcoat was dripping wet and his beaver hat was pulled down to cover his face. He scanned the bar, then strode to where Gareth was seated.

"Don't you think you've had enough?"

Gareth didn't have to look up to know it was Daniel. He knew the answer to his question, but he asked anyway. "Why? Do you have something new for me?"

"No."

"Then leave me alone," he said tersely.

Daniel ignored him, and pulled out a chair. "Didn't you tell her?"

Gareth's gaze narrowed to slits. He considered ignoring the question, but knowing Daniel's tenacity, the bastard wouldn't back down. "I did. She wants another man."

"I see."

No. He didn't. Gareth couldn't even understand what Jane saw in the pompous captain.

"I told her she'd regret it," Gareth said.

"How romantic of you. I'm sure that went over well," Daniel said mockingly.

"Go to hell."

"Not before you."

They sat in silence. "I'm taking you home. You have a trial tomorrow, remember?" Daniel said.

Did he? Another disgruntled husband. He couldn't even recall his client's name. Lord something or another. Poor sod.

Daniel shifted in his seat. "Do you want my advice?"

"No."

Once again Daniel ignored him. "I suggest you try to convince her. It's not like you to give up."

Gareth looked at Daniel for the first time since he walked into the tavern. "I told you she chose another man."

"Did you ask her why?"

Gareth was startled by the simple question. Jane never gave him a reason. He wanted something he'd never wanted before when it came to ending a relationship with a woman: understanding.

For the first time in his life *he* wanted a reason.

He needed to see Jane again. He'd pound down her door if necessary. Why hadn't he thought of it? Her interest in the captain made no sense. According to Jane's aunt, the captain wanted to marry. And Jane was adamant against marriage. She'd told him many times. Her marriage to the gambling earl was miserable and had ended tragically.

So what had changed her mind?

Gareth pushed back his chair to stand, but Daniel placed a hand on his shoulder and forced him back down.

"What the hell—"

"You're drunk. If you go to her late tonight, you'll accomplish nothing but to make a fool of yourself," Daniel said.

Gareth shrugged off Daniel's hand, but he stayed seated.

He knew his friend was right, but frustration felt like stab to his gut. He didn't want to wait. He wanted to see Jane.

Daniel stood and offered Gareth his coat. "I'll take you to your chambers, brew you a strong pot of coffee, and stay with you. After you've sobered, then you can go to your lady tomorrow."

Gareth jerked his fingers through his hair, pulling the roots away from his forehead until his scalp stung. Exhaling slowly, he dropped his hand. "All right. Let's go then."

• • •

The following morning, Jane halted at the sound of a knock on her front door. She'd been halfway across the marble vestibule on the way to the library when she'd heard the rapping. She glanced about for the butler, but not surprisingly, old Graves was nowhere in sight and probably hadn't heard the knock.

Her immediate thought was that Captain Turner had decided to pay a visit. She wondered if he sought an audience with Aunt Eleanor to discuss their engagement, or simply to spend time together. Her stomach clenched. She didn't want either to happen this morning. Her reaction was disturbing.

She planned to marry him, after all.

Another thought followed and her heartbeat quickened. She could be wrong and Gareth could be at the door. She quickly quenched the excitement running through her veins. She refused to think of him, and had sworn to stop acting foolishly. Gareth had made no effort to pursue her after she'd rejected his offer to continue their affair in Lady Vogleson's garden last night.

Taking a deep breath, Jane opened the door.

"Olivia!" Joy and relief rushed through Jane at the sight of her friend. "I didn't think you'd return for days."

Olivia stepped inside. "Edward and I were anxious to return for the remaining season. The countryside in Kent is lovely, but quiet."

Jane eyed her friend. "Quiet is the perfect place for newlyweds."

"Not if the Dowager Duchess accompanies the newlyweds."

"She accompanied you?" Jane asked aghast.

"We took her with us so that she could settle into the dower house. The problem is the dower house is too close to the main estate. We want our honeymoon to be about us. Our London town home is perfect."

Just then, Graves shuffled across the marble vestibule and took Olivia's pelisse.

"Some tea, if you please, Graves. We will be in the sitting room," Jane instructed.

Once the two women were ensconced in the sitting room, Jane shut the door and glanced at Olivia, noting the stunning pearl beading on her gown and matching pearl drop earrings and necklace. "Whatever the reason, I'm thrilled you've returned early. You look like a perfect duchess, and you glow with happiness."

Olivia giggled. "Edward is quite skilled in and out of the bedroom."

Jane felt her face grow hot. Not from Olivia's words, but from the image that immediately came to her mind of Gareth rising above her, his muscles in their naked glory, as he slowly made love to her. Sharing his bed had taught her more about pleasure than she'd ever dreamed.

Olivia studied her. "How are you, Jane? Please tell me

you've reconciled with Mr. Ramsey."

Jane sat on the sofa and waited until Olivia joined her. "I've something to confide in you, but you must keep it secret. I'm pregnant with child."

Olivia's mouth gaped. "But I thought…that is you told me…that you couldn't—"

"The doctor must have been wrong. Only my aunt knows and she swore to keep my secret."

"This is wonderful news. You've always wanted a child. Now you and Mr. Ramsey can marry."

"No, Olivia. We can't. Mr. Ramsey has no wish to marry," she said in a low, composed voice.

Jane didn't tell her friend Gareth's reasons. She wouldn't betray his secrets to another. He was a spy for the Crown, and he'd taken a risk to reveal the truth to her. She wouldn't tell anyone his secrets, even her closest friend.

"How dishonorable of him! What will you do?"

"I've interest from another man."

"Who?"

"Captain Liam Turner. He's older, but very respectable and in search of a wife. We are very suitable." He needed an army wife, and she needed a husband.

"You mean to pass the child off as his?" Olivia asked incredulously.

It was the efficient thing to do. She almost cringed at the choice of words that ran through her mind. She was beginning to sound like Captain Turner.

"Please don't think me a horrible person," Jane pled.

Olivia grasped her hand. "Never! Mr. Ramsey is the horrible one. You must act to protect yourself and the babe."

Jane didn't bother to correct Olivia. How could she

without revealing Gareth's secret? She accepted Olivia's sympathy and felt relief to have shared her condition with her friend.

All would be well now. It had to be.

• • •

Gareth was grateful for Daniel's interference last night. The tavern had been a close walk to his Gray's Inn chambers, and the cool night air had helped clear his head. Daniel had made him drink several cups of coffee and had stayed with him to ensure he didn't do anything he'd regret. He had slept on the sofa in his office and Daniel in one of the leather chairs situated in front of the desk. Gareth had been in a bad way and there had been a strong possibility he'd knock down Jane's door if she didn't answer.

After Daniel left, he went to the closet at the end of corridor where he always kept a fresh change of clothes. He knew he'd looked a fright with his rumpled jacket and disheveled hair, and he couldn't see Jane until he saw to his appearance. As he sat behind his desk tying a freshly starched cravat, his thoughts turned to the best way to approach her when Stevens knocked on his office door. His clerk's normally composed features were flustered.

"Her Grace, Duchess of Westmont, is here to see you, sir," Stevens said.

Gareth frowned. Olivia was here? He immediately thought of the duke and wondered if his reckless brother, William, was in trouble once again.

Olivia flew into his office, her voluminous skirts swirling around her legs. "You swine!"

Gareth shot to his feet from behind his desk. Her blue eyes were flashing, not in panic, but fury.

"Olivia, what in God's name—"

"It's Your Grace now," she said in an officious tone.

Gareth's lips twisted wryly. "Pardon, *Your Grace*. What is this all about?"

Her eyes blazed with anger. "As if you didn't know."

"I assure you, I have no idea what has riled your temper."

"Jane is pregnant," she snapped.

His mind reeled, and he felt as if he had been punched in the gut. "What did you say?"

"You heard me perfectly, sir. Lady Stanwell is pregnant with your child, and you refuse to act honorably and marry her."

He couldn't believe it. Olivia thought he knew. Years of experience as a barrister hiding his inner emotions aided him now. He stood still, not a muscle twitched in his face.

"How do you know?" he asked, his voice as steady as if he was speaking to a judge in a crowded courtroom.

"Lady Stanwell confided in me. She also said you have no wish to marry. How could you! I should have the duke call you out."

If the situation weren't so dire, Gareth would laugh. The duke wouldn't stand a chance against him. Years ago an experienced army sniper and client had paid him in shooting lessons, and Gareth was a crack shot.

"She's a lady and the widow of an earl. Just because society unjustly blamed her for her husband's suicide doesn't give you a right to abandon her. It's *your* reputation that's unsavory," Olivia said tersely.

She was right. Jane had done nothing to deserve society's

cruelty. As for his reputation, he understood. He was estranged from his father, the baron, and society believed it was due to his choice of legal expertise. His father was never looked down upon. Gambling was not only expected, but encouraged among the upper class. No one knew of Gareth's secretive activities on behalf of the Home Office.

Olivia tried to hurt him, but nothing she could say was more wounding than the fact that Jane had not told him herself of the baby.

But how could it be? She claimed she was barren. That a doctor confirmed it. She'd been married for three years to Lord Stanwell without conceiving.

Had she lied?

Why would she? She would undoubtedly face even more of society's cruelties if the child was born out of wedlock. It wouldn't make a difference to his standing in society or his legal career.

Except she wouldn't be shamed. She planned to marry Captain Turner. Pass the child off as his.

*Over my dead body.*

The child was his. No other man would give him his name.

Something shifted inside his chest. A painful tug of desperation. It wasn't until he was going to lose everything that he realized he loved Jane. The emotion he'd always scorned and mocked others for falling victim to had ruthlessly torn down his own defenses.

She'd upset his balance from the very beginning—since he'd first found her on her hands and knees in a library reaching for her wayward list of potential lovers. Since then he'd come to admire her ability to survive her unhappy marriage as well as her strength to survive society's cruelty after her husband's suicide.

From an early age, he'd been hurt by his father's neglect and gambling addiction. He'd learned not to trust or need or to rely on others. Espionage fit him well. The rules were simple. Never get emotionally involved, never trust anyone. Emotion meant weakness and could result in failed missions and disastrous consequences.

And then Jane had entered his life. It had ceased being about the mission a long time ago—long before she'd shared his bed. He'd buried his feelings for Jane because he'd feared them. But the startling truth was he *needed* her. He needed her spirit, her laughter, her very essence.

And she was going to marry another man.

"Well," Olivia said, hands on her hips. "What are you going to do?"

Gareth walked around his desk. "I assure you that there's no need to involve the duke. I promise you that I'm going to speak with Jane and remedy the situation. Tell no one."

# Chapter Twenty-Eight

After Olivia departed, Gareth paced his office. He was fearful and furious—a volatile combination. With a swipe of his arm across his desk, papers scattered to the floor.

Stevens immediately appeared in the doorway. "Are you all right, sir?"

"Cancel my appointments for today." Gareth instructed as he snatched his coat from the coat rack. "I won't be coming back."

Concern etched Stevens's features. "Yes, sir."

Gareth made it to Piccadilly in record time. He banged on the front door with a fist.

Jane's elderly butler opened the door. Upon seeing Gareth, he cleared his throat. "Lady Stanwell is not—"

Gareth slapped a large hand against the door, preventing the butler from shutting it in his face, and stepped into the vestibule. "Summon your mistress," he ordered. "I'll wait in the sitting room."

The butler gaped as Gareth strode past him and down the hall. Gareth's emotions were a whirlwind as he paced the Oriental carpet until he heard footsteps outside the sitting room. At last the door opened and Jane entered.

She looked beautiful in a simple morning dress of blue alpaca. She was pale, with faint circles beneath her eyes. He felt a stab of worry.

"What are you doing here?" she said.

His fingers itched to reach out and touch her, to pull her into his arms. "I had a most interesting visit from the duchess this morning."

"Olivia?"

"Yes. She says you are pregnant with my child."

Jane paled a shade more. Then she laughed, a high trill of sound. "Don't be ridiculous. We know that's impossible."

"Do we? Because Olivia had no doubt as to what you said."

She turned away, and Gareth's control snapped. He grasped her arms and pulled her to him. "Tell me the truth, Jane."

"There's nothing to tell."

He shook her, and her head fell back to gaze into his eyes. "Don't lie to me."

Her eyes grew very large. "I didn't believe it myself at first. There was the doctor's prognosis. But it must have been Charles who couldn't…who wasn't able to…"

"Go on."

"All the signs are present. I haven't bled, and I've been so nauseous lately."

"It's true then," he prodded.

"Yes. It's true." Her voice was a mere whisper.

He couldn't believe it. Hearing it from her lips was a

shock all over again. A bitter sense of betrayal welled within him. He cursed and released her abruptly.

. . .

Jane took a step back at his anger. He was furious about her pregnancy. She'd been right; he clearly didn't want the babe.

"And you planned on passing my child off as another man's?" His voice, though quiet, had an ominous quality.

He knew. Somehow he knew everything.

An unwelcome tension stretched ever tighter between them. "I saw no other choice."

His jaw bulged. "No other choice? How about advising the child's *father*?"

She swung on him. "To what end? You don't want to marry."

He stared at her with dark, desolate eyes. "Neither did you."

A heaviness centered in her chest. "It's no longer solely about my desires or needs."

"You're right. It's not."

The chill between them seemed to grow. She bit her lip. "You don't have to worry. I won't seek anything from you. I have plans to care for the child."

"How? By marrying Captain Turner?"

She tried not to flinch. "What does it matter to you? You needn't worry about a scandal. No one will know."

"After all this time, do you think I would avoid responsibility and deny my own child?"

She blinked at the forcefulness of his tone. "I…I don't know what to believe."

A flicker of emotion crossed his face. Pain? Regret? But

it was gone so swiftly she thought she imagined it. "Why didn't you tell me? You don't want the child, do you?"

Her heart pounded, and her sorrow was a huge painful knot inside her chest. He had no idea how badly she'd prayed for a child of her own. Years of despair married to a man she thought she loved only to lose him to his gambling addiction had taken its toll. After Charles's suicide, she'd been left with nothing.

Absolutely nothing.

Jane touched her stomach. "The child is a miracle to me. A miracle and a blessing. I want the baby very much."

The tension in his face eased. "Then marry me."

She shook her head regretfully. "You don't have to do this."

"Why do you refuse me?"

"You claim to be an agent for the Home Office, a spy who works for King and Country, a man who doesn't want to marry because of the danger surrounding your espionage assignments."

"That was before. It doesn't matter now. None of it matters. I'd give it all up."

"But it does matter! I've lived through a marriage where my husband didn't want me. He'd acted *dutifully* by fulfilling his family's demands. It was an empty and lonely life, and I refuse to be the unwanted wife once again." She stopped short in dismay and searched his face. "Can you honestly say that you won't regret your decision years later? Or, worse still, that you won't resent me and the child for giving it all up?"

"Never. Despite what society says about me, I am an honorable man."

He mentioned honor, not love.

*Don't be a fool,* she thought. Captain Turner never mentioned love either. But the problem was she didn't love the captain, whereas her heart ached for the man standing before her.

"Say yes, Jane."

She choked back tears and shook her head numbly.

The door opened and Jane whirled to see Aunt Eleanor. If she was shocked to see Jane alone with a strange man, she didn't show it. Instead her aunt looked genuinely pleased.

"Mr. Ramsey. How nice to see you again," Eleanor said.

Surprise siphoned through Jane. She looked from her aunt to Gareth. "When have you two formally met?"

"On Bond Street. Your aunt was kind enough to tell me you were attending Lady Vogleson's ball and that a certain army officer was courting you," Gareth said.

Jane stood stunned at the knowing look that passed between the two of them. What on earth had her aunt been up to?

A second knock on the door sounded. It had been left ajar from when Eleanor entered and Graves appeared in the doorway.

"Captain Turner is here to see you, my lady," Graves announced.

The captain! She'd completely forgotten about his scheduled visit. They were to walk in the park together.

A quick look at Gareth's fierce features, and she knew an instant's panic. She feared a fight between Gareth and the captain.

Jane took a step toward the butler. "Please tell Captain Turner I'm indisposed and to return another—"

"No," Gareth cut her off. "Please see the captain in," he said. His tone was light, but Jane wasn't fooled.

Graves looked from one to another, uncertainty etched on his wrinkled face.

"I say listen to Mr. Ramsey," Eleanor chimed in.

Jane gaped at her aunt. "Why in heaven's name did you say that?"

Eleanor pointed her cane at Jane. "The quicker this is resolved the better."

The thought of Gareth and the captain together in her sitting room was outrageous. Nothing good could come of it—especially now that Gareth knew the truth. What on earth could her aunt be thinking? Jane considered fleeing to her bedroom.

Too late, Captain Turner walked into the room.

Jane felt nerves flutter in her stomach as the captain came to a stop in the center of the Oriental carpet. He stiffened when he noticed Gareth and Eleanor.

"Am I interrupting something?" the captain asked.

"Yes," Gareth said.

"No," Jane said.

Captain Turner frowned as he looked at Gareth. "Do I know you, sir?"

Gareth faced the captain and his grin did not reach his eyes. "Not yet, but you will. I'm Lady Stanwell's fiancée."

Jane gasped.

Captain Turner's lips thinned as he tugged on his coat. "What's the meaning of this? The lady and I have an understanding."

Gareth turned to Jane, a wry gleam in his eye. "Should I tell him? Or will you?"

She felt her face drain of color. Gareth meant to tell the captain of the pregnancy, not the engagement. She had no choice.

Jane took a deep breath and looked up at the captain. "I'm afraid I cannot marry you, Liam."

Captain Turner blinked. "What?"

"I'm sorry." She shifted uneasily on her feet and was at a loss of what else to say.

The captain turned to Eleanor. "We had spoken."

"We never agreed. Jane is not a minor and does not need my permission. And there was no reading of the banns," Eleanor pointed out.

"But I was to get a special license," the captain protested.

"Have you?" Eleanor asked.

The captain's brow furrowed. "Not yet, no."

"Then there is no harm done." Aunt Eleanor thumped her cane with finality that said there was no need for further conversation upon the matter.

"No harm! The lady's behavior is abominable," the captain shouted.

Jane opened her mouth to protest, but Gareth cut her off. "Careful, captain. I think you should leave."

The man's face turned blotchy. Eleanor was quick to go to the captain's side. "I shall walk you out."

"I can walk myself out," the captain said tersely.

He whirled and left the room. Footsteps sounded and seconds later the front door slammed shut.

Jane stood stock still.

"Goodness!" Eleanor said. "He turned quite unpleasant."

"Did you expect otherwise?" Jane asked incredulously.

"I expected better of an army officer," she huffed. "I

shall leave you two alone to discuss details."

As soon as Jane was alone with Gareth, she whirled to face him. "How could you? I had no choice but to turn Captain Turner away."

"I saved you. He would never have made you happy."

"And you can?"

"Yes. No one else can bring forth your passionate nature."

"I've told you before, lust is not love."

"It's a fantastic start."

She was so angry she wanted to hit him. Her gaze fell on a pitcher resting on an end table. He must have sensed her intent for he grasped her hand and tugged her to him.

Her body sizzled where it touched his.

"You have to marry me, Jane."

"No, I don't." The command wasn't the proposal she had dreamed of. She knew she was acting irrationally, but this was not what she wanted.

"You would have our baby out of wedlock?"

It was his tone that made her lip quiver. The stark hurt in his face. She swallowed. "I had hoped for…well, more."

"What? Tell me and you shall have it. I'm a wealthy man. You and our child will never want for anything."

"I'm not speaking of money."

His eyes lit with understanding. "Don't you know by now? Can't you tell by the way I'm acting? I love you with all my heart, Jane."

The last of her defenses crumbled. "Oh, Gareth. I've loved you for so long now."

"Truly?"

"Yes, truly." Reaching out, she stroked his cheek. "But what of your work for the Home Office?"

"I was serious when I said nothing else matters. You don't believe me, do you?"

"I don't want you to have regrets."

"There's only one way I can show you."

He kissed her with a tenderness that melted her bones. He held her like fine china and got down on his knee. "Please marry me, Jane. Make me the happiest of men." Then he kissed her belly and she felt a relief so profound she dropped to her knees beside him.

All would be well. Their baby would know only love.

Aunt Eleanor cleared her throat in the doorway. "Well it's about time," she said, wiping a tear from her eye.

# Epilogue

Daniel strode into Gareth's Gray's Inn chambers. "I heard you are being considered for King's Counsel."

Gareth crossed his arms behind his head and leaned back in his office chair. "I hope to hear soon."

Things had changed over the past months. Gareth was now an advisor to the Home Office, just like his friend Robert had become after his own marriage. He continued to maintain his chambers and work as a barrister, but he no longer represented disgruntled husbands and handled different civil matters.

His working life had changed.

But most importantly, he'd married Jane.

They'd been married by special license in the Duke of Westmont's elegant drawing room. Olivia and Daniel had stood as their witnesses. Aunt Eleanor had cried throughout the entire ceremony.

Gareth's espionage assignments may have ceased, but he'd gained so much more. True to his word, there wasn't a day he missed the dangers of spying. His advisory position more than fulfilled any need to aid the Home Office and Crown.

"I've come with news of my own," Daniel said. "I want to resign as undersecretary and take on more of a role as a spy."

Gareth suppressed a laugh. "You're tired of clerical duties?"

Daniel sat on the chair in front of Gareth's desk. "Why should you and Robert have all the fun?"

"We're both finished with the day to day dangers of espionage, remember? We're married men, and I have a child on the way."

"Heaven forbid I fall in love," Daniel said dryly.

Gareth chuckled.

"Sir Marbury finally passed away. The Marbury Company has been sold off. Simon hasn't been heard of since his banishment to the Continent," Daniel said.

A knock on the office door drew their attention. Stevens opened the door to hand Gareth a note. "There's a message from your wife, sir."

Gareth unfolded the foolscap and read the single sentence in Jane's handwriting out loud. "It's time."

His heart jolted as the true meaning of the message registered. Gareth jumped to his feet and dropped the paper. "Good God! The baby's coming."

"Go man," Daniel said.

Gareth made it to their home in record time. Jane was pacing in the hallway outside their bedchamber. Aunt Eleanor was by her side.

"Why aren't you in bed?" he asked.

"My water broke an hour ago. The contractions have started, but I'm told it could take a long time," Jane said.

"We've sent for the physician," Eleanor said.

Gareth walked with Jane until the contractions came faster and harder. When she gasped in pain and rubbed her low back, he swept her into his arms. "Let's get you in bed."

The contractions were relentless and increased in intensity and duration along with the pain. Gareth sat at Jane's bedside and held her hand.

"You should leave," the physician instructed Gareth.

Jane whimpered and shook her head.

"I'm not going anywhere," Gareth said. "She needs me now more than ever."

Sweat beaded on Jane's brow and she turned frighteningly pale. Her grip on his hand tightened as the contractions banded unmercifully around her belly. Gareth had never felt so helpless and feared she couldn't take much more.

Eight hours later, he would have gladly taken the pain upon himself. He bathed her forehead with a cool cloth and whispered words of encouragement in her ear.

At last the physician announced it was time. With one last push and scream from Jane, the baby came with an infant's cry.

"It's a girl!" Eleanor said.

Gareth stared in amazement at his daughter. He counted ten perfect tiny fingers and toes. "A baby girl," he whispered, his throat hoarse with emotion. When Jane smiled and reached for their baby, he swore she never looked so beautiful.

Afterwards, when Jane wore a clean gown and the baby suckled at her breast, he couldn't keep his eyes from the pair.

Jane looked up and a wrinkle appeared on her brow. "No regrets, Gareth?"

Gareth dropped to his knees beside the bed and smoothed her forehead. "Never. I'm the luckiest man alive. I'll love and treasure you both forever with all my heart."

# Acknowledgments

I'm eternally grateful for my readers. Without you there would be no books!

Thank you to my wonderful agent, Stephany Evans, for her feedback and constant support of my work. A special thank you to my editor, Alycia Tornetta, who helped polish the book and make it shine.

Thank you to Laura and Gabrielle for being supportive and giving me time to write. A special thank you to my family and Jeannie and Fran for their help so I can attend conferences and meet my readers.

# About the Author

Best-selling author Tina Gabrielle is an attorney and former mechanical engineer whose love of reading for pleasure helped her get through years of academia. She often picked up a romance and let her fantasies of knights in shining armor and lords and ladies carry her away.

*A Spy Unmasked* and *At the Spy's Pleasure* are books in Tina's newest series, *In the Crown's Secret Service* series. She is also the author of adventurous Regency historical romances, *In the Barrister's Bed, In the Barrister's Chambers, Lady of Scandal*, and *A Perfect Scandal* from Kensington Books.

*Publisher's Weekly* calls her Regency Barrister's series, "Well-matched lovers...witty comradely repartee." Tina's books have been Barnes & Noble top picks, and her first book, *Lady of Scandal*, was nominated as best first historical by *Romantic Times Book Reviews*. Tina lives in New Jersey. She loves to hear from readers. Visit her website to learn about upcoming releases, join her newsletter, and enter free

monthly contests at www.tinagabrielle.com.
You can also find Tina on Twitter and Facebook.